I0582759

HFCA Publishing House

Ireland

ISBN 978-1-918152-10-4

www.lexibuchanan.com

First Published 2017

This version 2025

Copyright © 2017 by Alison Higson

Proof Reader: Lynne Garlick

Alison Higson asserts the moral right to be identified as the author of this work

This novel is entirely a work of fiction.
The names, characters and incidents portrayed in it are the work of the author's imagination. Any resemblance to actual persons, living or dead, events or localities is entirely coincidental.

All rights reserved. No part of this book may be reproduced in any form or by any electronic or mechanical means, including information storage and retrieval systems, without written permission from the author, except for the use of brief quotations in a book review.

Chapter One

"AUNTIE MACK, ARE WE THERE YET?"

I look in the rear-view mirror, and see my nephew, Lucas, becoming increasingly restless. It makes me smile. Even after just thirty minutes, the "are we there yet?" inquiries have begun. "Not just yet, but we shouldn't be too far off. I promise."

He lets out a dramatic sigh before staring out of the window.

I pretend not to be amused while at the same time my heart is warming up to the thought of him. Since the moment my sister gave birth to him, he has always held a special place in my heart; now he is six years old and full of mischief. Because his mother Melinda and father Daniel have a flight to Europe scheduled for later in the day, Lucas had opted to spend some time with me in Cape Elizabeth.

I've been working for most of my life, and this past spring, I treated myself to a summer rental by splurging on Rose Cottage.

My parents, who are matchmakers and want to see me married with a child of my own, will definitely be surprised by this new development. I'm only in my twenties, so I have no clue what all the fuss is about when it comes to this topic.

My train of thought is once again interrupted by a long, heavy sigh coming from the backseat. I am prepared for what is to come...

Three... Two... One...

"Are you sure that we haven't arrived yet?" Again, Lucas inquires while wriggling his fingers.

As I respond to Lucas, my amused lips twitch slightly as I say, "Lucas, we'll be there soon. You have a lot of books, so why don't you read one of them?"

"I'm sorry, Auntie Mack, but my books are dull. Could I have one of yours to read?" The very idea of it makes him so giddy that he practically jumps up and down in his seat.

"My books are intended for adults, and as such, they do not contain any illustrations." It is a relief to know that my books are safely tucked away in the trunk, where Lucas cannot access them.

"Daddy told mommy that she would learn a lot more if she read the kind of books you read rather than the dull magazines that she currently reads. I like to learn," Lucas says with his 'cute' face.

When Lucas gives me that look, I have never been able to keep anything from him, so my eyes start to fill with amusement. He is obviously hoping that I will give in to his demands and allow him to root around in the box containing my belongings. The more I think about it, the more embarrassed I become, and I start to wonder what kind of books Daniel thinks I read. "You can't read them unless you're an adult, Lucas. If you're getting tired of yours, I'll gladly buy you some new ones once we arrive at our destination."

"As soon as we get there? You promise?" The books that Lucas is currently reading are tossed onto the empty seat next to him.

"In a day or two, we'll go check out the stores." I take a quick glance in the mirror and notice that Lucas's face has started to become more serious. As a result, I say to him, "But if you're good until then, I'll buy you that atlas you wanted, and then you can keep track of where your parents are staying in Europe."

After giving my words some thought, Lucas gives me a reassuring nod and smiles. "That would be pretty cool."

"Why don't you try getting some rest? When we get there, I'll make sure you're awake. That way, the time will pass super quick."

After another five minutes, Lucas is sound asleep, and after an hour and a half have passed, I pull up in front of Rose Cottage and turn off the engine. Lucas must have been startled awake by the calm and silence because he suddenly sits bolt upright in his seat and slams the side of his head against the window with a dull thud. "Lucas, are you okay?"

He rubs his head. "I think so. Are we there yet?"

"Yes, we are, thank goodness... Let's stretch our legs." When I look over to the other side of the yard, I see a man ambling towards us at a casual pace. He has a slight build, is of average height, and his dark grey hair is cut short. As he draws closer, I see the wind and sun have taken their toll on his weathered face, which is bronzed. "As a matter of fact, I believe I can see Mr. Degan making his way to the cottage." I assume that the man to the left of me is the landlord for the summer.

I climb out of the car and open the back door for Lucas. In his excitement, he leaps out of the car and circles me several times before sprinting off to meet the proprietor of Rose Cottage.

As I watch Lucas dash toward Mr. Degan, I have a sudden change of heart and decide to go over to them instead because I have no idea what Lucas will say when he gets there. "Mr. Degan?" I question, offering my hand. "My name is Mackenzie Harper, and this is my nephew, Lucas Cartwright."

After he has finished releasing my hand, Mr. Degan asks, "You like fishing?"

"Um, not really." My eyebrows furrow in confusion. There is no welcome; there is only fishing. I have absolutely no intention of getting anywhere near the bait, and the prospect of removing the fish from the water does not appeal to me either.

"I wasn't talking to you, young woman. I was having a conversation with this here boy." Mr. Degan directs his attention to Lucas.

The motions that Lucas makes resemble those of an excited puppy. "I've never gone fishing before, but Daddy says you should try everything once."

"Mmm, the river has some big suckers in it," the man says. "I figured I could catch something with you as the bait?"

While Lucas appears to be perplexed, I feel like my own eyes are going to fly out of my head. "Mr. Degan, I don't . . ."

"Take a deep breath. I am merely playing a joke on you. Please refer to me as Thomas. Even though I'm in my eighties, whenever you refer to Mr. Degan, it makes me feel like my father."

I gave a small smile and shift gears. "Do you have the keys?"

Thomas responds, "No need. The doors open." Along the way, he's accompanied by Lucas, who, as we approach the cottage, puts his hand in Mr. Degan's. Lucas seems instantly at ease with the older man. As for me, I'm not really sure how to approach Mr. Thomas Degan.

In the kitchen is where I finally catch up to them. It is nothing at all like what I had envisioned after reading the online description of it. But it's a pleasant surprise. It's spacious and bright, and the white cabinets, give it a classic look. The countertops seem to be made of a beech wood that is not too old. Linoleum with a pattern in yellow and white is used for the flooring. A flowery ceramic jar with cooking implements poking out of it sits to the side of a large wooden chopping block. Also nearby is a hanging rack that is stuffed with pots and pans. It is safe to say that I do not miss the coffeemaker that was situated next to a wooden stand that featured hooks for storing coffee cups.

As I move to the stove to take a closer look at it, I make the conscious decision to exercise some caution before I even attempt to turn it on. The stovetop appears to have been thoroughly cleaned, and it looks very similar to the one in the home in which I grew up in.

When I turned around to face Thomas again, I ask, "Have you always lived around here?"

He scratches his chin. "Around the year 1924, my parents made the journey from Ireland to this country in order to start a new life here. They initially settled in New York, but in 1927 they made the move to Rose Cottage in this very location. It goes without saying that everyone called it "Degan House" back then, including me when I was a kid."

"Perhaps you could spare some time and tell me more about your parents? Come over for coffee and homemade cake?" I really hope that Thomas will be tempted by the food that is being offered.

He removes the cap he wears. "Hmm."

Thomas is pleasant, particularly given the fact that he doesn't appear to mind Lucas hovering. In point of fact, it seems as though Lucas has made a new friend.

"Thomas, if you'd like to join us for dinner, I have pizza in the cooler, and there's plenty of it; in all honesty, it's too much for the two of us to eat by ourselves."

As soon as Thomas sits down on the worn-out stool in the kitchen, Lucas immediately jumps up onto his lap. "Please stay, Mr. Degan."

"Don't mind if I do," Thomas responds while grinning in my direction. "If you give me permission, I'll keep this little jumping bean entertained while you unload the car. I'm afraid I'm too old to do the unloading these days."

"I can manage, and it would be wonderful if you could keep an eye on Lucas for me."

As I stand outside, I turn my head and take in the breathtaking scenery, which includes the ocean, the cliffs, and the cylindrical dome-topped lighthouse that is perched on the edge of the headland. The light at the top of the dome flashes as it rotates.

Bright splashes of color can be seen all around the cottage; there are roses in both red and yellow, marigolds, cone flowers, and sunflowers. Trees and bushes that bloom in the spring and offer snowball-sized bursts of blue and white hydrangea as well as heavy purple cones of fragrant lilac. The season of summer is represented by trellises that are covered in flowers.

Planters and hanging baskets provide even more splashes of color when they are displayed on a porch that goes around the entire house. The back of the deck is lined with Adirondack chairs, all of which face the water.

At the very end of the garden is where you'll find a gazebo, which provides a perfect spot to take a seat, get some shade from the sun, and keep an eye on Lucas while I read a book or enjoy a cup of coffee in peace and quiet.

As I take a long, deep breath of the clean, salty air, I can't help but feel relieved that, unlike most days in the city, I won't have to worry about inhaling a lungful of car fumes in the process. Not only does everything have a clean aroma, but there is also a euphoric lack of noise. No honking horns from passing vehicles, and no loud neighbors. The only sounds that can be heard are the birds singing, the wind in the trees, and the waves lapping against the shore. To me, it is nothing short of paradise.

I start unloading the car with a spring in my step and make a few quick trips back and forth as I carry Lucas's toys, our clothes, and books into the quaint cottage.

The final trip inside is to bring the food, and it isn't until after I've put everything away in the cabinets and the refrigerator that I realize how peaceful the cottage is. Lucas is six—he doesn't do quiet.

As I listen, I hear voices coming from the upper floor.

After securing the lid of the cooler and getting it ready to be loaded back into the vehicle, I head down to the bottom of the stairs to grab a box of clothes and then proceed to the upper level. After hastily putting the box in the room that I believe to be the master bedroom, I open one of the doors on the landing and find both of them seated on one of the twin beds that occupy the room. To Lucas, who is beaming with glee, Thomas is currently reading what appears to be an extremely vintage comic book.

As soon as Thomas spots me, he raises the comic to his face and starts laughing. "Lucas discovered it beneath the closet, where he also discovered a few spiders."

I try to calm my nerves by looking around. "Spiders?" I inquire of Thomas, who is laughing.

"I believe it would be best if I left you two alone for the time being. I'll let you know as soon as dinner is ready by giving you a shout."

I haven't stopped looking for spiders even after I've closed the door, and I hear Thomas and Lucas laughing as I make my way downstairs.

I'm such a wimp!

"THOMAS! LUCAS! IT'S TIME TO EAT DINNER!" I YELL from the kitchen. "Please wash up."

After messing around with the antiquated but spotless oven for a while, I was finally successful in producing a nicely warmed pizza.

I cut it into small triangles of a consistent size and then arranged them in a pattern on a plate for serving. As soon as Thomas and Lucas make their appearance, I place the pizza and potato salad on the table.

"Please have a seat. What would you like to drink, Thomas?"

He responds, "Water's fine," as he helps himself to pizza and potato salad while we are talking.

After I've given everyone a drink of water, I go over to the two boys who are still hungry.

"Have you and your family always called Boston home?" Thomas inquires while stuffing his mouth with pizza.

"Yes. Born and bred there, Roslindale specifically."

Before turning to face Thomas, Lucas flashes a grin. Suddenly, he blurts out, "She's a schoolteacher, and she scares all of the children in the classroom."

"Lucas, if you could please refrain from talking with your mouth full, thank you."

Indignantly and with a sly grin, Lucas responds, "You and Mr. Degan just did,"

"Well, Mr. Degan and I are very naughty then, so you behave." I chuckle.

"Is she always going to be this bossy?" Thomas shows a grin.

While shoveling in more food, Lucas says, "You really have no idea," while simultaneously speaking around a mouthful of food. "You really ought to count your blessings that she is not your aunt."

"Hey, if you want to go back to Boston, I can always drive you there. You can stay with your grandparents," I say sternly, suppressing my laughter.

"No way. They are old and no fun. They don't want to do anything else but play cards all day long." As soon as he sees the frown forming on my face, he continues, "And strip poker."

I feel my cheeks heat up and begin to blush as I choke on my drink. "They do no such thing, young man. Well, maybe cards." I turn my head to look at Thomas, who appears to be struggling to eat without laughing.

The things that occasionally come out of Lucas' mouth are so funny that it's hard not to laugh at him.

The remainder of the meal is consumed in a relaxed and unhurried manner, and before I realize it, Thomas has finished clearing the table and is beginning to load the sink with water and dishwashing liquid.

"Thomas, you don't need to do that." I stand to help.

"I'm aware that it is not necessary for me to do this, but I still want to. Why don't you get some coffee started?" he asks, a glint of mischief in his eye.

I can't help but laugh as I go to do what he wants. While I'm waiting for the coffee to brew, I decide to follow Lucas into the living room and turn on the gaming system that I set up for him while waiting for the pizza to cook. Before going to bed each night, he is allotted thirty minutes of free time.

After I've finished drying the dishes, I go and sit down with Thomas at the kitchen table, where I'm hoping he won't mind if I ask him about his history. I find it very interesting to learn about other people's lives, particularly before and immediately after the Second World War, and I am already at a point with Thomas where I feel comfortable enough to ask him questions about his life.

"Would you mind if I asked you about your family, specifically about your parents? What were they like? What did they do?" Thomas gives the impression that he has never had that question asked of him before. "I find family history rather interesting," I add.

He frowns and looks into the cup of coffee he is holding. "My mother and father, hmm. My mother, Josephine, and my father, Thomas, were both born in Delgany, which is located in County Wicklow, Ireland, in the year 1899. They immigrated to the United States in the early 1920s on the RMS Mauretania, which traveled from Southampton to New York."

"It's been a lifelong dream of mine to go to Ireland but getting there would require a flight that's quite a bit longer than I'm comfortable with. Have you, Thomas, ever been there? There must be some of your family still living there?"

"I believe there is, but I wouldn't know them if they jumped out at me. I have never communicated with them, and I don't believe that either of my parents, maintained relationships with any of their family after moving here."

"What did your parents do for work?"

"After they had arrived, my father was offered a good position with a law firm in Portland. This happened after they had settled in. Because the company paid well, the family relocated to this area in 1927. They started out by renting this cottage for a few years before eventually purchasing it. Even during the height of the Great Depression, my mother never held a job; instead, she spent her time socializing with her friends and sipping tea. My father was constantly busy with work. He was known to have a short fuse. He used to scare the crap out of me."

We take a sip of our drinks.

"Were you their only child?" I inquire with an utter sense of fascination.

"No. Charlie was my older brother. He died toward the end of the Second World War, and a sister...she died a few years later. My mother passed away in 1951 from a heart condition, and my father did the same in 1964. When my father passed away, we hadn't been in contact for years, so it came as a shock to find out that he'd left everything to me. It was at that time that I decided to change the name of the cottage." He exhales loudly, his eyes showing signs of weariness as he does so.

"I'm grateful that you took the time to tell me about your family. You have a remarkable capacity for remembering dates."

"I've always been good with figures," he responds in the affirmative. "I think I'll just call it a night."

I keep an eye on Thomas and as soon as he stands, I say, "Please come join us for breakfast."

His wrinkled and weathered face breaks out into a gleeful smile. "I have other obligations in the morning, but I will call on my way home." He walks out without saying anything else, and the only thing that breaks the silence is when Lucas bursts into the kitchen.

"I overheard you inviting Mr. Degan to breakfast; do you think it would be alright for me to sleep on the sofa tonight while I wait for him to return?"

I give a gentle chuckle as I lead him to the upper floor. "It's not necessary for you to sleep on the sofa because I believe that you will be awake well before he arrives after breakfast." While I start the water for his bath, I look over at my nephew, who is currently leaning against the doorjamb and smile to myself.

He grunts and groans and mutters to himself, as if he believes that I'm completely oblivious to what he is saying. I have listened to each and every one of his gripes about how adults are bossy.

I turn my head and grin as I practice my facial expressions. "If you want to see Mr. Degan in the morning then I suggest you run and get your pajamas. We'll put them on the heater so that they're nice and warm for when you get out of the bath." Because Lucas has already sped off to his room in such a hurry, my words are rendered meaningless.

After breathing in all of that ocean air, hopefully he'll be able to get some rest.

Chapter Two

"AUNTIE MACK, AUNTIE MACK, IT'S TIME TO GET UP."
Lucas yells as he bursts into my bedroom and takes a
few seconds to get on the bed. "Come on, Auntie. You
have to wake up. The birds told me that it's time to
have breakfast." He takes a moment to catch his
breath. "They want pancakes, and they want ketchup."

I rub my eyes and pull the blanket away from my
face as I slowly open them. I take one look at my very
excited nephew, and then it finally registers that I just
heard him say pancakes and ketchup in the same
sentence.

"Lucas, you don't eat pancakes and ketchup
together. That's, uh, not the way things are done." I
take a quick glance at the clock that's sitting on the

side table and then rub my scratchy eyes. I really need glasses because I'm sure the clock reads not much past five. I'm rubbing my eyes once more. "Oh, my goodness, Lucas, it's only ten minutes after five in the morning. Nobody gets up at this time." I lean my head back against the pillow, grab hold of Lucas, and assist in getting him tucked in alongside me under the covers. "Okay, it's time to go back to sleep... Please?"

"When can I get up?" Lucas asks.

"I'll rouse you in a couple of hours." After turning my head to look at him, I'm relieved to see that he is already deeply asleep.

"ARE YOU REALLY, REALLY SURE THAT I CAN'T HAVE ketchup with my pancakes?" Lucas complains while maintaining a glum expression.

"No, Lucas, ketchup does not belong on pancakes. Ever. It was designed to be used on fries, which is why syrup was developed to be used on pancakes."

In the midst of our intense eye contact, I place a glass of chocolate milk and a bottle of syrup on the table next to his plate and proceed to stare him down.

"Wow, chocolate milk," is what he cries out in amazement. "Syrup is good."

I make sure that Lucas can't see the grin that's spreading across my face as I turn my back on him. I need to avoid doing anything that might encourage him to act cheeky, not that it seems to make much of a difference.

As I take a seat, the first mouthful of mouthwatering coffee slowly makes its way down my throat.

Following breakfast, I accompany Lucas into the living room, where I turn on a game for him to play for a brief period of time. "Don't have it turned up too loud, okay?"

"I won't." He cracks a grin, clearly already preoccupied.

I stand back and let him finish up while I make my way over to the bookshelf that is located on the opposite wall in the living room. I take one of the old hardbacks out and blow the dust away in order to read the title, 'Gone with the Wind.' My jaw drops when I realize I'm holding a first edition.

"Why would such a book be left in a summer rental?" I mumble something to myself as I tinkle with the worn bound cover of the book. As I slide it back into place on the shelf, I can't help but wonder what other hidden treasures lay behind the layer of dust that has accumulated there. However, before I can investigate further, there is a brief knock on the door. Thomas walks in just as I'm about to respond. "Morning, Miss Mackenzie. I hope you were able to get a good night's sleep."

"I did, thank you."

Lucas rushes into the kitchen as I follow at a slower pace.

"I was wondering if you could let me take care of the boy for a couple of hours?" Thomas inquires while pulling a chair out from under the table and then removing his weight from his feet.

I need a few moments to think about this because, despite the fact that I have the impression of knowing Thomas for a long time, I don't really know him... While I consider what he has asked of me, I ask him, "Would you like coffee?" because I know that going with him won't be a problem for Lucas at all.

He nods and then takes off his cap.

After pouring a cup of coffee for both of us, I take a seat next to him. "I was wondering if you were aware that there is a first edition of Gone with the Wind sitting on the bookshelf in the living room."

Thomas gives a gentle smile. "It was a book that belonged to my mother, but it was the one that my sister read the most. Because of this, it has not been removed." He gives a shrug. "In regard to taking Lucas..."

"What do you have planned for today?"

"I was thinking that I have a lot of those comics, like we were reading yesterday, in a box in the garage," he says. "Lucas could lend a hand in bringing them inside so that we can go through them together."

"What a charming idea. By the look of things, Lucas would love that."

"Let me go and wash up once more. I'll be back in a moment." Lucas dashes up to the bathroom on the second floor.

The level of enthusiasm he displays causes me to burst out laughing. "I would like to thank you, Thomas, for the conversation we had last night. I found that listening to be very enjoyable. I sincerely hope you didn't think I was prying into your business."

"I haven't really talked about them in a very long time, and I quite enjoyed sitting here, drinking coffee while I talked about them with you," he says.

"I'm glad. When you left, I couldn't help but feel a twinge of concern in case our conversation about them had upset you."

He gives a light head shake. "That happened a very long time ago. I have no problems discussing them now."

I nod. "Are you certain that having Lucas won't bother you in any way? He can be quite a handful at times." The frown deepens. I'm a lot younger than Thomas is, and with the amount of energy that Lucas has, he could probably wear out a lion. Heaven alone can count the number of times that he has worn me down.

"You shouldn't be worrying yourself. In the event that there is a problem, I have your mobile phone number, and I only live five minutes down the footpath."

On his reappearance, Lucas slips his hand inside Thomas's much larger one.

"Bye, Auntie Mack."

"Bye, Lucas. If you want to have any chance of being invited back, you need to act appropriately."

Lucas grins with his gapped teeth. "I will."

"I'll see you later, Thomas. And I want to thank

you once more." I watch as they make their way down
the footpath hand in hand.

"Mr. Degan," Lucas asked. "When were these
comics first published? There is a significant amount
of dust." He sneezed.

Thomas laughed and coughed at the same time. "I
have owned these ever since I was a young child. I
first used my allowance to purchase them in 1942,
and I believe I continued to do so for a period of
approximately five years." He looked upset. "Why
don't you call me Thomas?"

A grin appeared on Lucas' face as he continued, "Thomas."

"That's all there is to it." Thomas beamed a grin as
he observed the child's expression of pure joy.

"Would it be possible for me to take a peek inside
this one?" The question was posed by Lucas, who was
brandishing a comic book with a rather gory cover.

"That is a special edition for Halloween. Please
have a seat, and I'll get you some milk and cookies in
a moment."

"Yummy." Then he snapped back to his proper manners. "Thank you."

Thomas made his way into the kitchen while racking his brain for the last time he had this much fun. Sadly, he was unable to. Janet, his wife, passed away when both of them were fifty-six years old. It had been twenty-four years since then. They hadn't been blessed with children of their own. Because Janet had been an only child and both of Thomas' siblings had passed away many years ago, he did not have any nieces or nephews; rather, he was an honorary uncle to the children of his friends whom he had become close with over the years.

It had been far too long since he'd had a kid over to his house for a visit.

I HADN'T REALIZED HOW MANY BOOKS I'D ACTUALLY brought with me until I unpacked them and arranged them in neat piles on the top shelf of the closet, in the hopes that Lucas won't be able to reach them. During this time off, I'm going to try to get through at least half of those books. Lucas is only going to stay with me until his parents return.

After disassembling the boxes, I drag a chair to the kitchen counter, climb up, and cross my fingers that there are no spiders before carefully stacking the flattened boxes on top of the wall cabinets. The sound of a thump and the fact that the boxes do not slide into place make me frown. After lifting the boxes and looking underneath, I discover what appears to be a book of some kind, although it is completely obscured by a thick layer of dust. I reach for the book, and then quickly lay the boxes down before I jump back to the floor. I grab a clean cloth and wipe away the thick layer of dust that has accumulated on the cover.

When I pick up the ancient book, the hairs on the back of my neck stand on end because I have a passion for history. It appears to be quite outdated and suggests that it has been in that location for quite some time. Before turning to the first page, I give the front cover of the supple book with the leather binding a light stroke.

This is the diary of a Rose
March 4, 1947

"Oh, my." I get into a seated position on a kitchen chair. Stunned. The diary was kept for...seventy years, and who exactly is Rose? Why is she keeping her journal on the counter above the kitchen cabinets? My interest is so piqued that I can hardly contain it. After the passing of his parents, Thomas gave the cottage its name—a relative?

"Auntie Mack, I'm home!" Lucas yells, entering the kitchen in a hurry.

The revelation that the diary was there has set off a frenzy of excitement within me. I certainly don't want Lucas getting wind of what I've found. He would look everywhere for it so that he can check it out for himself if he discovers it.

Thomas follows behind Lucas, and glancing at me, frowns. But as soon as he sees what I'm holding in my hands, his face goes completely blank.

I keep a close eye on him and then I ask, "Thomas, are you familiar with anything about this book? It was written in 1947 and it says, "This is the diary of a Rose." Could it have been a relative?" As I wait for his response, I conclude that Thomas may be in a state of shock. "Thomas, are you feeling all right?" As my anxiety increases, I move closer.

"Yes, yes, fine. I need to get home." He makes a move in the direction of the entrance.

"But wait a minute, isn't this yours? After all, it is the cottage that belongs to your family."

Thomas has now completed his turn and is looking at me. "It's all right, you found it, so read it first and then give it to me to look over. I hope you have a pleasant evening."

After that, there is no sign of him anywhere.

THAT EVENING, BEFORE I HEAD DOWNSTAIRS TO prepare a steaming cup of hot chocolate, I make sure Lucas is asleep. Even though I've already showered and changed into my pajamas, I just can't get my mind to settle down for the night.

As I stir the hot milky drink, my mind keeps going back to the diary that I found earlier in the day. Within those pages is the story of somebody's life, and the revelation of that fact fills me with excitement. When I think about Thomas's reaction when he heard Rose's name, I can't help but frown. What had that been about?

As I take another sip of the hot chocolate and

make my way upstairs to the bedroom, my thoughts begin to drift away. As I settle into bed, I keep the door to the room slightly ajar so that I can listen for Lucas. After that, I take the journal in my hands and open it to the first page.

Chapter Three

This is the diary of a Rose . . .

March 4, 1947

    My name is Rose Degan, and I am 19 years old.

This is my first diary.

    After the events of yesterday, I have decided I must keep one.

Yesterday was a very exciting day in Cape Elizabeth, and in my life, because I met the most handsome man . . .

I WAS CURRENTLY WORKING IN THE HISTORY SECTION OF the town library, where I was responsible for dusting the books and the shelves. It was without a doubt the worst possible assignment that my boss, Mr. Young, could give to anyone, but for some reason, he seemed to enjoy assigning it to me.

At the nine-minute mark, my brother JT came running around the corner, and I was on a ladder. He almost knocked me off it. Because he was so out of breath, I began to feel panicked. "JT, what is it? Is everything okay?" I enquired while frantically searching him from head to toe for any signs of injury.

"Sis, will you take me to watch the rescue at sea?"

"What in the world are you talking about?" JT had a reputation for making up stories every once in a while.

"Walt reported that a collier ship was unable to navigate the storm and ran aground at Two Lights. I beg you, are you going to take me?"

I could tell Mr. Young a harmless fib because it was not as if I was extremely busy right now, and the dust would still be there the next day. Having made up my mind, I grabbed JT by the hand and left him for a short while with Emma before going in search of Mr. Young to inform him that I was sick with a 'female' problem.

I left his office a short time later, grinned to myself as I went. The reaction of my boss was exactly what I anticipated it would be. First, his face turned as red as a tomato, and then he slumped down into his chair. He looked like he was about to pass out. He most likely hoped that I wasn't about to reveal any additional information.

After hastily gathering my belongings and JT, the two of us set off in the direction of Two Lights alongside a large number of the town's inhabitants.

As we got closer, we could hear cheers coming from everyone. It sounded more like a celebration than a search and rescue mission.

A friend from school named Sarah could be seen standing not too far away with her older sister. As soon as she noticed us, we began to make our way over to them, which proved to be quite challenging due to the fact that JT was attempting to pull me in the opposite direction.

JT pulled on my hand and said, "Sis, I want to go over there to see Walt and Levi," for the umpteenth time.

"Give me a moment while I find out what's going

on by first speaking with Sarah. Then I'll take you over there."

I didn't pay any attention to JT as he moaned and groaned about why he always had to do what the adults told him to do.

"Sarah, what exactly is going on?" I asked, after we'd finished hugging each other. Sarah was the kindest of people, and she embraced everyone she met. At first, she would make me feel awkward, but now that I'd gotten used to her, I found that I enjoyed the familiarity.

"They launched a breeches buoy to the vessel, and at this time they are rescuing members of the crew. Everyone claps and cheers whenever they successfully bring another person to shore."

"I wonder if they require any assistance," I commented at large. Matilda, Sarah's sister, who was always so prim and proper gave me a dark glare.

Finally, after about ten minutes of polite conversation, I allowed JT to steer me toward Levi and Walt, his two best friends and, on more than one occasion, partners in crime.

While I did my best to keep an eye on JT, the air was still a little bit chilly, and gusts of wind kept wrapping around me and tossing me around. There was already a sufficient amount of chaos; there was no need for JT and his friends to contribute to it.

When I turned my head to look around, I saw a very good-looking man staring at me. I stilled, and at that precise instant, every sound vanished, and the two of us were the only ones in this location. Unfortunately, I quickly came to my senses when he started walking toward me with a nonchalant grace, which caused my heart to flutter wildly in my chest.

He had a face that exudes an air of intellectual allure. Because of his imposing shoulders, the coat that he wore was completely filled, and his stance drew attention to the strength of his thighs and the narrowness of his hips. The way that a section of his dark brown, wavy hair fell carelessly across his forehead lent him an air of boyish charm.

As he stood in front of me, his eyes were locked on mine, and they brimmed with attraction. His lips twitched slightly. "Hello," he said, the chocolate smoothness in his voice came through clearly. "I haven't seen you around here before." When he smiled, his teeth stood out against his tanned face.

"I'm Rose." I greeted him nervously by holding out my hand to him, and the moment our palms touched, I got the sensation that I'd been hit by lightning. It appeared that he was taken aback as well, judging by the look of surprise on his face.

He cleared his throat. "Jacob Evans. It's been just about a month since I moved to Cape Elizabeth. Do you live in this general area?" His eyes had me completely enthralled.

"Not far away, and in close proximity to the beach. I'm employed here in town, at the public library."

JT came running over. "Sis?" He alternated his gaze between the two of us. "What the heck is going on? Why are you talking to him?" he asked while pointing at Jacob. "You're supposed to be marrying Richard, you can't talk to him."

The hasty comment made by JT hurt. Even though he was only a teenager, I really wished I had the power to silence him, especially now that he'd brought up Richard. Ugh. Brothers!

I quickly glanced over at Jacob to see what reaction he had to the statement made by my brother, and I saw disappointment cross his features as he released my hand and stepped back.

JT, whose impatience was really starting to irritate me, said, "Rose, come on."

"It's probably best if I go with him," I said. "I hope

to see you again." JT was finally successful in dragging me away.

"I hope so," he said with a tinge of longing in his voice.

Before I lost sight of him completely, I cast a glance back, only to find his eyes locked on my retreating figure. My heart hadn't slowed down from its frantic pace yet.

"Sis, now that you're engaged to Richard, you really shouldn't be having conversations with random men."

"JT, I will not marry Richard, not now, not ever, and one day Mother and Father will understand that."

Jayne, my very best friend, stopped by the house after dinner to see me. I yanked her around the corner and made her sit in the garden. I didn't want anyone else to hear what I had to say to her, but by the end of the evening, I'd wishing I'd kept it to myself because she told me I was being stupid. That it was impossible to develop feelings of attraction for someone you had only just met.

March 8, 1947

Richard came calling today . . .

SINCE THE LAST TIME I SAW JACOB, IT HAD BEEN FOUR days, and every time I took a stroll through the town, I found myself looking for him. Why hadn't I inquired as to where he was employed? I informed him that I worked at the library; however, it was possible that he didn't want to see me, which caused me more distress than it should.

My mother had been trying to get me to focus on Richard even though I'd been spending most of my time daydreaming about Jacob. Richard was the only child of Bernard and Evelyn, who also happened to be the owners of a number of businesses in the area, including the local newspaper, a hotel in Boston, and a few other local enterprises. Because of this, it came as no surprise that my parents thought him an excellent catch. My mother did not seem to grasp the concept that the reason I wanted to get married is because of love, not because of money or status.

Richard was a tall, blond-haired man with blue eyes; however, he was more interested in tinkering with cars than he was in me, or in anyone else for that matter. Actually, I found him to be quite boring. On each of the two dates I'd had with him, I'd been counting down the minutes until I could get back home. I'd only agreed to go on them to stop my parents from bothering me about him.

Today, I was attempting to conceal my location by snoozing in the hammock in the garden. Mother was allergic to virtually everything that could cause an allergy; as a result, despite the fact that she adored the garden, you would never find her actually working in it. She was not going to put herself through the ordeal of breaking out in hives in order to locate me. At the very least, I really hoped that she wouldn't.

"Rose, what are you doing in here?"

"Richard?" I was on the verge of tumbling out of the hammock because of him. "What are you doing here?"

"It shouldn't be a surprise that I'm here to see you," he replied.

What was it about that response that made me feel anxious?

He assisted me in getting out of the hammock and led me to the bench that was located inside the recently constructed gazebo.

"Rose, how are you doing?" He looked anxiously around the garden while shuffling his feet nervously.

"I'm fine. I'm grateful that you asked. "How are you?" I loathed polite conversation with a passion.

"Good, good." He started to walk in a circle in front of me, going back and forth.

"Richard... I beg you to halt." As I watched him, I found myself saying, "You're making me dizzy. What the heck is wrong with you?"

He stopped walking in circles and then uttered the one word that I was desperately hoping he did not say. "Marriage."

I immediately shoot up to my feet and stand in front of him. "I beg you not to propose marriage to me. Please. We don't even know each other."

"It's what both of our parents want." He moved away from me and sat down on the bench before turning his attention to the ocean and appearing to be deep in thought.

"Richard, do you love me?" I was waiting for his response as I stood to the side of him.

He looked at me. "No."

I let out a sigh of relief. "I don't love you either, and if I ever marry, it will be because of love, not because of our parents," I told him. "That ought to be one of your goals as well. You can't possibly expect to be content if you don't have romantic feelings toward your spouse, can you?"

He grabbed my hands and pulled me down onto the bench next to him. "Oh, Rose, I cannot tell you how much I appreciate your candor with me. I concur with what you said. My current priorities do not include getting married and starting a family. In point of fact, I think it's about time that I take charge of my own life rather than constantly having it directed for me. However, I would treasure the opportunity to call you a friend."

I raised a grin to his face. "Friendship would be lovely," I said with some degree of relief.

Chapter Four

THE FOLLOWING MORNING AS WE MAKE OUR WAY toward the beach, Lucas takes off running ahead the moment he sees Thomas's cottage in the distance.

I make my way up the flight of four steps. "Good morning, Thomas. I'm sorry to interrupt, but I think Lucas has something important to discuss with you."

He relaxes his head and laughs as he does so. "Oh, yes, I am aware of that." His eyes twinkle. "Lucas asked me if I wanted to come to the beach with him to watch you," he coughs, trying to disguise a smile, "skinny dip."

I had just taken a swig of bottled water, which resulted in water dripping down the front of my shirt. "He never?" I look first at Thomas, and then over at Lucas, who has an evil grin on his face. "Did he?"

Thomas gives a small nod to the side.

I squeeze my eyes shut. "Lucas Cartwright!"

"Granny goes skinny dipping," Lucas says in his defense.

I give Thomas a fleeting look, and he appears to be on the verge of laughing out loud. I let out a sigh, and then I switch gears. "Lucas, it's time for us to leave because we're going to the beach. Would you be interested in coming with us?"

Thomas looks from my face, which is reddening, to Lucas's face, which is hopeful. "I believe that I will." After that, he gives Lucas a knowing wink and continues, "Providing that your auntie keeps her clothes on. Might give me a heart attack at my age."

Lucas starts giggling.

As soon as Thomas appears on the scene wearing his lightweight jacket, Lucas grabs both of our hands and directs us toward the beach. Once we've arrived, I lead us to a spot where there's some shade. "Let's take a seat here so we don't end up looking like lobsters. Do not believe that you can get away with anything, Lucas, because I will still be able to keep an eye on you."

While sitting next to me on the blanket, Thomas makes the observation, "He sure is a handful."

I laugh. "Oh, he is for sure. It seems to me that he pays too much attention to his grandmother. I pull my legs up and rest my chin on my knees. "Thomas, this place is beautiful. It's hard to believe that in all the years I've spent in the Boston area, I've never made it out to Cape Elizabeth... It's incredibly calm and serene here."

After a few moments have passed, Thomas gives me a sideways glance before returning his attention to Lucas. "I've never lived anywhere else," he says. "During the years that we were married, my wife Janet and I traveled all over the world, visiting places such as Europe, Canada, and Australia. However, ever since she passed away, I haven't gone anywhere. After looking at what I already have and realizing that I have this in my own backyard, I see no reason to go anywhere else."

"It's paradise, Thomas."

"That it is." The focus of Thomas's gaze comes to rest on me. "Can I ask you a personal question?"

I give a wary nod while wondering what kind of question he is going to ask next.

He leans his head to the side as he waits for a

response before asking, "Why don't you have a boyfriend?"

I immediately meet his gaze, and then blush because the question takes me by surprise.

He has a chuckle. "You're quite the looker for such a young lady, Mack. Even though I'm getting on in years, I haven't experienced any problems with my eyesight.

"I date, but—"

"No one has ever lit a spark?"

"I believe that about sums up everything."

"When you finally do meet the person with whom you are destined to spend the rest of your life, you will understand." He smiles. "As soon as Janet gave me a smile, I knew she was the one," he says. "She is the only person who has ever captured my attention in the way that she did. Her grin could make a dark room seem bright." Lost in his thoughts, I give him space.

I let out a sigh as I look out across the ocean while I take pleasure in Thomas's company in the peaceful silence...until Lucas comes crashing down onto the blanket with a bang.

He stretches out his arms and leans against

Thomas's side, rubbing his eyes before letting out a huge yawn.

"Are you sleepy, Lucas?" I ask.

He starts to nod off as sleep overtakes him.

Thomas adds, "I think I'll have a nap as well," while he spreads out next to Lucas on the ground.

"Well, if the two of you are sleeping, I'll go ahead and read." Before I go and get Rose's diary out of my purse, I wait for them to finish getting comfortable on the blanket.

After leaning against a small rock and watching a yacht far out in the ocean until it disappears over the horizon, I finally open the diary to the page that I had bookmarked earlier.

Chapter 5

March 11, 1947

We meet again . . .

My day off from the library was today, and I was
very much looking forward to seeing Jayne while she
was in town. Since I first met Jacob, I'd spent a lot
more time worrying about how I looked, just in case I
ran into him again. If I did, I wanted to make a good
impression. It had been seven days since we first met,
and I seem to be looking for him everywhere I go. I
thought this was because of how much I missed him.
I sincerely hoped that he was still in Cape Elizabeth.

As I made my way toward 'Belle's Tea Rooms' to meet Jayne, it was thirty minutes after the midday hour. Belle was originally from Cornwall, but she relocated to the United States after the war so that she could be with her husband, whom she had married while he was stationed over in England. I couldn't even begin to describe how incredible her scones and cream cakes are, which was why I was so excited for our treat each month.

After giving a quick glance up the street in search of my friend, I didn't see any trace of her, and then I heard my name being called from behind. When Jayne waved, it made me smile.

"Rose!"

"Jayne, I'm glad you're not late again." Whenever Jayne and I made plans to meet, she was invariably going to be late by at least ten minutes, which forced me to stand around and wait for her.

"Let's get inside. I haven't had lunch yet." It wasn't unusual for Jayne to arrive here without having eaten lunch first. She made up for it with the cakes.

When we opened the door to Belle's brightly lit entryway, the first thing that greeted us was an aroma that was absolutely irresistible. My eyes immediately traveled across the room to the display of cakes, but the moment they landed on Jacob, everything inside of me came to a complete and total stop. Because Jayne was preoccupied with what she was saying, she walked directly into my back, which forced me to move toward Jacob, who had walked across the room and was holding both of my hands.

"Rose," he muttered in a low voice. "I can't believe... Rose, you're here?" He seemed to be waiting for me to vanish before him as he held my hands tightly in his.

"Rose, who is this?" Jayne asked.

Since I'd located Jacob once more, I'd totally lost track of the fact that Jayne was with me. "Jayne, I want you to meet Jacob. Jacob, my best friend, Jayne."

Jacob smiled and said, "Nice to meet you, Jayne," without taking his eyes or hands off of me as he spoke. "Please join us?" Jacob extended the invitation, and before I had a chance to respond, he was already guiding us across the room to his friend. When I saw the other woman, I experienced a brief moment of hesitation. He hushed me and whispered, "She's my sister," while giving me a knowing smirk.

"Eleanor, I would like you to meet Rose and her friend, Jayne."

Eleanor raised an eyebrow on hearing my name.

Remembering his manners, he pulled a chair out for me, and then he did the same for Jayne. Jacob and I were looking at each other wistfully while Jayne and Eleanor had a conversation.

"Are you really sitting in front of me?" Jacob muttered, unable to conceal the yearning in his voice.

"I thought it was going to be the last time I saw you," I confessed. "I thought maybe you had already left Cape Elizabeth."

It appeared that he was going to caress my face, but at the last second, he pulled his hand away abruptly. "I couldn't for the life of me remember where you worked." He had a chuckle. "I looked for you all over town and tried to find you in so many different places."

I took his hand. "I'm employed at the library. I've been looking for you as well."

Before I knew it, our tea and cake had been consumed in its entirety. While Jayne, and Eleanor made their way toward the restroom, Jacob grabbed my hand and led me into an alcove that was hidden by a really large potted plant.

"Will you assure me that you are not going to marry that other man?"

"I'm not marrying him," I replied.

When he leant in and gave me a gentle peck on the cheek, I was completely taken aback. "Can I see you again?" He moved closer.

"Yes," I responded, unable to catch my breath and hoping against hope that my heart wouldn't leap right out of my chest.

Then, whatever peace I had left is shattered from the hunger of his kiss, which only lasted for a few seconds, leaving me in a whirlwind of emotions. I wanted more.

Jacob's observed me intently. He must like what he saw because he grinned, broadly. "Can I see you tonight?"

"Oh, yes," I enthusiastically responded.

I told him where I lived, and we immediately made plans to meet on the beach at 8:30 this evening.

Jayne didn't stop talking about Jacob and how much she worried that my parents would disapprove of our relationship the entire way out of town. I made it clear to Jayne that it was my life, and that I would visit Jacob whenever I felt like it. She seemed to be in a bad mood as she stormed off. I was not going to let anyone know about him from this point forward. I most certainly did not want my parents to learn about him before I'd spent more time with him.

My father was a snob, and in his opinion, anyone who did not go to work dressed in anything other than a suit was not worthy of his one and only daughter. My mother was the only one he had ever loved. The fact that he viewed my work at the library as a source of irritation was all the more motivation for me to continue doing it.

In the later hours of that day, I gave my hair a good brushing so that it would shine. I put on one of my brand-new dresses, which was a delicate shade of pink and featured white piping around the collar and the cuffs. I started off by putting on my pink lipstick, and then I slid my feet into my pink shoes.

As I quietly sneaked out of my room and made my way downstairs, through the kitchen, and finally out the back door, I felt butterflies in my stomach due to the excitement.

I sneaked through Mother's rose garden and through the opening in the hedges to the beach path. After five minutes, I came around a bend in the path and saw Jacob, who was grinning broadly as he reacted to seeing me for the first time.

I quickened my pace and Jacob started walking toward me at the same time; before I knew it, we stood face to face.

Before he brought his lips to mine for the most tender of kisses, he reached out with his hands and gently stroked my face with the palms of his hands.

"I simply cannot fathom the fact that you are standing right in front of me. That I am currently pressing my hands against your face. I feel as though I've known you for years and that it hasn't only been a few days since we met," he confessed.

Tears welled up in eyes. "I understand what you're saying. I feel the same, Jacob."

Before taking a step back and taking my hand in his, he composed himself. "Rose, please come. Let's go for a stroll along the beach before it gets completely dark."

"I'd like that."

We walked along the sandy beach wrapped in each other's arms, his warmth as our bodies brushed together caused a blush on my cheeks.

In the past, I had gone out on dates with other young men; during those dates, we had walked hand in hand down the beach and through the streets of town, but none of those dates had ever made me feel as good or as right as being with Jacob did.

Was I developing feelings for him? In all honesty, I

was very content in my relationship with Jacob, and I had been from the first.

While we strolled along the beach, he filled me in on everything there was to know about his sister, Eleanor, as well as how close he was to her.

Even though she was ten years his senior, the two of them had been inseparable throughout their childhood. Before the war, she had been engaged, but her fiancé had been killed in France toward the end of the conflict. It appeared that she hadn't been the same since then, and she continued to feel a deep longing for him.

The number of people who had suffered the loss of loved ones as a result of the war is brought home to me by him. Including my family.

All too soon, it was time for me to head home before I was missed.

"Rose, I don't want to lose hold of you. Please don't. How is it possible for that to happen after only a couple of meetings?

I mumbled, "I feel the same," as I pressed my face into his chest.

He placed his hand under my chin and tilted my face in order to bring his lips closer to mine. He did this very gently.

"Would you be willing to have lunch with me tomorrow? On the grass in the middle of town?"

"Yes." I quickly turned around and started running toward my house before I remembered that we hadn't agreed upon a time, so I turned around and shouted, "One o'clock."

He responded, "I'll be there," while waving his hand.

March 12, 1947

I can't wait for lunch . . .

I HAD SPENT THE ENTIRE MORNING WATCHING THE clock inching its way slowly closer to one in the afternoon. When excited about going somewhere else, why did the passage of time seem to move at such a snail's pace?

"Rose?"

Mr. Young.

"Yes?"

"I have been speaking with you for the past five

minutes, but it seems as though you are only physically present here. Are we keeping you from something?"

"I wouldn't say that. Is this the end of the meeting?"

I left in a hurry, paying no attention to Mr. Young's confused expression as I go. Before I left the library to go meet Jacob, I made sure to grab my coat and purse from the staff room.

As I ran along the sidewalk toward the green, I could hardly contain my excitement. When I arrived at the large grassy area in the middle of town, I was greeted by mature trees and winding paths. People were taking advantage of the beautiful weather, dogs were pulling their walkers behind them, and a few kids were having fun playing tag and Frisbee. Wild animals could be seen grazing along the perimeter of the small pond that was located in the middle of the green.

As I got closer to the covered pavilion, I didn't have to look very hard to find Jacob. I took a moment to gather my composure and noticed that my heart was beating faster than usual as a result of the sight of him. It was hard for me to comprehend how important he had become to me. I even gave my arm a light pinch once or twice to make sure I was not having a dream about it.

He went through the motions of pacing back and forth before pausing to take in his surroundings. Was he tense up there? Worried that I wouldn't turn up? Once more, he lifted his head and his eyes landed on me. He stopped moving, and a broad grin broke out across his face.

I lost control of my body and ran toward him, throwing myself into his arms. He gave me a very intense hug.

"Rose, I can't tell you how much I've been looking forward to seeing you again. This morning, thinking about you made it impossible for me to concentrate on anything else." After gently stroking my face, he moved his fingers down to my neck and shoulders.

"I've spent the entire morning keeping an eye on the clock," I must own up to it, sheepishly.

Jacob gave me a friendly smile, took my hand, and led me down the steps to the grassy area below. Before putting his arm around me, he assisted me in settling into a comfortable position on a wooden bench.

"There is only about twenty minutes left for me. Lunch breaks aren't all that lengthy here."

"Twenty minutes with my Rose is better than none at all."

I felt completely satisfied as I laid my head on Jacob's shoulder. Jacob and I could sit together the whole day in complete silence, and I would still be well aware of his presence.

"Rose, are you willing to share with me a little bit more about who you are?"

After giving my watch a quick glance, I noticed that fifteen minutes had passed while the two of us had been preoccupied with our own thoughts. "I'm not entirely certain we have enough time, but I'll let you know there is also my brother, JT, as well as my parents. In addition to that, we have a housekeeper who does her best to keep JT in line, but unfortunately, she fails more frequently than my parents would like." When I thought of my prankster brother, I couldn't help break out in a warm smile. "I believe that it's time for us to leave."

"I know. I'm having trouble moving. I want to spend the entire afternoon holding you in my arms. I'm really falling for you, Rose," he gulped, appearing to be very vulnerable.

"I'm falling for you too...but I need to get back. My job isn't something I particularly enjoy doing, but it drives my father crazy." Jacob chuckled at the same time as I did.

He was the first one to stand and was extending his hand to me. As soon as I placed my palm against his, he immediately grabbed hold of my hand and leant in for a kiss.

Jacob pulled away and pressed his forehead against mine as he took a strand of hair from my head and twirls it around his fingers.

My heart pounded extremely fast in my chest, and I had butterflies flitting around in my stomach as a result of the way he looked at me. It was almost as if he wanted to eat me.

"I can't see you again until Friday, but I want to take you dancing. Rose, would you like to come dancing with me?"

I responded immediately with, "Yes," and enthusiastically nodded my head.

Once we were back on the sidewalk, we discussed the best time and location to get together on Friday, and then we parted ways. Both of us then proceed to walk away, but in opposite directions.

Chapter 6

THE NEXT MORNING, AS I LAY IN BED THINKING ABOUT Rose and Jacob, I listen to the sounds of the birds chirping outside the window.

Given that the name of the cottage is "Rose Cottage," it does not take a lot of creative thinking to deduce that Rose is the person for whom the cottage was named. She also has the same last name as Thomas; could she be his sister? Thomas had stated that he had changed the name after the passing of his father. He referred to a sister who had passed away. It would most definitely explain Thomas's response to seeing the diary if this were the case.

I am perplexed, so I shift the quilt to the side of

the bed and climb out. After a speedy shower, I get dressed and then head down the hall to check on Lucas before beginning to prepare breakfast in the kitchen downstairs.

Not even five minutes later, Lucas asks, "Auntie Mack, when will Thomas be here?"

When I turn around, I see Lucas standing in the doorway. He is completely dressed, and the water from his morning shower is still on his face. "I had no idea you were awake, and I'm surprised you've already showered and dressed." I try to cover up my grin. "He is expected to arrive later on today. Come and have some food."

After Lucas has taken a seat, I set his breakfast on the table in front of him. "Hot cereal... Are you absolutely certain that's how it's supposed to be made?" As he puts his spoon into the bowl of white mush, Lucas asks with a look of disgust on his face.

"You're right, Lucas, this is hot cereal. Combine it with some syrup or natural yogurt and see how you like it."

"I'm not sure if I like eating hot cereal."

"Be thankful that I didn't include any prunes or apricots in your portion." While I am putting yogurt and syrup in my own bowl, I force myself to suppress my laughter at the horrified expression on his face.

"Oh, my goodness. Could we have something more substantial to eat... maybe a burger for lunch?" Lucas whines.

"If you eat your breakfast, we'll find some greasy food for lunch as a treat on the way back from shopping." I can't help but laugh as I watch him quickly shovel his breakfast into his mouth while making a face of disgust with each spoonful that he puts in. "You're going to get a stomachache if you don't slow down." I give a satisfied shake of the head while smiling warmly.

ONCE WE'VE GROCERY SHOPPED AND PURCHASED SOME books for Lucas, I pull into the driveway of Rose Cottage to find Thomas stepping up to the front of the cottage.

I open the door of the vehicle for Lucas, and he immediately jumps out and runs over to Thomas to tell him all about the water fight that took place in the grocery store as well as about the fact that we stopped for actual food on the way home. From the sound of Thomas's laughter, I can infer that he found the situation to be just as amusing as I did.

There was no damage done, despite the fact that as the responsible adult I should have included a reprimand somewhere in what was said. In addition, it seemed as though each of the parties involved was equally to blame, so I chose to ignore it.

"Thomas, I was wondering if you'd be interested in coming in for a glass of lemonade." I inquire as I take a hold of one of the shopping bags from the trunk of the car.

He then helps me into the kitchen by saying, "Don't mind if I do," as he opens the door for me. After following us into the kitchen, he takes a seat in what seems to be his preferred chair in the vacation rental cottage. After that, he makes himself comfortable and invites Lucas to sit on his lap.

The question he poses to Lucas is, "Can you swim, boy?"

"I can swim two hundred meters without stopping, and I have a badge at home to prove it," boasts Lucas with a sense of accomplishment.

"Good, because I was thinking, if you didn't have

anything planned this afternoon, I might take you fishing with me for a couple of hours if it's okay with your aunt."

"That's not a problem. He participates in swim team practices three times a week at his hometown, where he is known to be an excellent swimmer."

So that I can have a private conversation with Thomas about the journal, I turn to Lucas. "While Thomas is finishing up his lemonade, I think it would be best if you went and played your new game."

As soon as Lucas enters the living room, Thomas immediately turns his attention to me. While he takes another sip of his drink, he asks, "Something on your mind, Miss Mackenzie?"

"To begin, why don't you just refer to me as Mack?"

He nods.

"You know who Rose is, don't you?"

Suddenly, he pushes himself to his feet and places his cup on the table in front of him before making his way over to the window. "I haven't brought her up in conversation in the past seventy years, and I have no plans to start doing so now. He exclaims in a frantic tone, "It's time to go fishing!"

I was taken aback by the nature of the response to

my inquiry, but I will avoid further discussion of the matter...at least for the time being.

"THOMAS, WHAT'S IN THAT TUB?" LUCAS ASKED because he could see something moving inside it.

"Bait."

"I thought I was bait." Lucas paused. He was bewildered and asked, "What's bait anyway?"

"When a fish tries to take a bite out of the bait that is attached to the end of the line, it becomes entangled on the hook that is holding the bait because the fish like the flavor of the bait." When Thomas saw the look of shock on Lucas's face, he couldn't help but laugh.

"You're not really going to use me as bait, are you?" Lucas took a few steps backward.

Thomas was roaring with laughter to the point where he needed to sit down in order to prevent himself from falling over. Tears ran down his face, and every time he looked at Lucas, he started laughing all over again.

"Oh, my dear boy," he said with a chuckle while dabbing at his eyes with a tissue. "I don't know when the last time was that I laughed so hard."

Thomas was successful in regaining control of his actions. "You're safe, Lucas. Please take a seat next to me, and I'll demonstrate how to bait a hook."

After taking a seat, Lucas awaited Thomas's instruction as he explained fishing techniques, including how to bait a hook, for the next ten minutes. Lucas was disappointed that he couldn't test it out on his own, but Thomas was concerned that his little fingers might get caught in the hook.

While Thomas and Lucas relaxed and waited for the fish to bite, Thomas offered Lucas a cheese sandwich and a glass of homemade lemonade.

"How long have you been fishing?" In between sips of his lemonade, Lucas asked.

Thomas casted a quick glance in Lucas' direction before leaning back against a tree and reminiscing about the time his father went out of his way to buy him something during the summer, rather than delegating the task to his mother or the housekeeper. Lucas was visible in the distance. "For my eighth birthday, my father surprised me by purchasing a fishing rod for me. That happened roughly seventy-two years ago at this point. I went fishing with my two best friends, Levi and Walt, throughout the entirety of that summer."

While Thomas was talking, Lucas continued to eat his cheese sandwich. After a moment, it was clear that Lucas had given some thought to what Thomas had just told him, as he then asked, "Are they still your friends, or have you had a fight? I get into fights with my friends on a regular basis."

Thomas let out a chuckle. "Oh yes, we're still friends, even though back then we were more like partners in crime because we used to get into all kinds of mischief together," he said. "I was grounded a lot when I was younger."

Thomas strolled to the bank of the river to check the line, and after doing so, he turned around to look at Lucas, who was staring intently in his direction. "I'll never forget that after one fishing trip, we were walking back to my house when we saw my neighbor putting some shoes out on the porch. It was right as we passed by. We hid ourselves behind some bushes, and as soon as she went inside the house, we crept up to her front porch and hid fish in three of her shoes. During that day, we caught approximately eight fish total. I seriously doubt that we will ever be so fortunate again. It was the only time my father ever laughed at one of my shenanigans, but he put me in time out for a week because of it. After he had finished correcting me, I could hear him laughing as he closed the door to my bedroom and headed downstairs."

Lucas giggled. "I think I need to pee."

Thomas appeared to be rather startled and expressed his hope that he wouldn't require any assistance. "Are you all right going behind that bush?"

"You mean I get to pee outside?"

Thomas made a show of nodding his head while suppressing an attempt to laugh.

"Yeah!" Lucas disappeared in the cover of a bush.

"Don't get too far ahead of yourself, Lucas."

"I won't. I'm peeing now."

"Okay, buddy." As Thomas watched the fishing line being cast out across the water, he couldn't help but let out a chuckle.

After a moment, Lucas caught up with Thomas. "I feel better now. I'd really appreciate it if you could get me one of those chocolate bars."

"Yes, you can. First, let me help you clean your hands with a wipe, and then I'll give you some chocolate. "

Not too much longer after that, Lucas's bobber

began to bob up and down on the water as the line performed an erratic dance back and forth. They both leap to their feet and howled with glee, and in their haste, they came dangerously close to losing all of their belongings in the river. Thomas was successful in bringing in a yellow perch while Lucas was jumping up and down and cheering.

"Well done, Lucas. Would you like to give it another shot to see if we can land enough fish for supper?"

"Yes. Auntie Mack is able to prepare them. It's possible that you'll have to empty out the insides first because she's a girl and is likely to scream and run away if she saw them. That's what I remember Daddy saying, in any case."

"Are you sure about that?" Thomas attempted to cover up his grin.

~

AFTER SPENDING ABOUT AN HOUR BAKING, I WRITE A note and tack it to the back door. This lets Thomas and Lucas know where I am in case they get home before I do.

After resolving that issue, I take a stroll along the

same beach path that Rose had used so many years ago. As soon as I get to the beach, I look around at the few bright beach towels that have been laid out on the sand by parents who are watching their children play. I make a U-turn and head for the cover of the rocks, all the while wondering if the two people who are in love have ever laid claim to this section of the beach.

Chapter 7

March 14, 1947

I put my dancing shoes on . . .

THIS EVENING, I WOULD FINALLY GET TO SEE JACOB, and I could not wait! I could hardly contain my excitement because he was going to take me dancing and he was going to meet me at the end of the driveway.

The door to my bedroom was opened by my mother exactly five minutes before it was time for me to leave the house, and she asked me why I was wearing such a big smile. I ignored her and told her that I was thinking about something Jayne had said earlier in the day. Of course, I didn't take her seriously. I was so preoccupied right now that I didn't even care if she believed what I said or not.

As I got closer to the end of the driveway, I looked around for Jacob but didn't see him anywhere, which made me wonder what time it was.

I stepped onto the sidewalk and looked in both directions, but I couldn't find any trace of him. I concluded that it would most likely be in my best interest to wait away from the road in case anyone I knew saw me and began questioning what I was doing...or even worse, asked my parents what I was up to. Ugh!

I was about to take a step back when arms encircled me, and his lips brushed against the base of my neck. "Hello, Rose," he murmured, and the sound of his voice sent chills down my spine.

I allowed myself to become more at ease in his presence and turned my head ever-so-slightly to kiss his lips. I mumbled, "I've missed you, and I've been looking forward to this evening so much."

"Me, too." He spun me around so that we could properly embrace one another. "We had better get going if we don't want to miss the bus."

Jacob did not let go of my hand until I had handed my jacket to one of the cloakroom attendants at the dance hall.

"Hey Rose, how about we start off with a drink?"

"No... Please take me in your arms and dance with me. I beg you."

As he dragged me onto the dance floor, his eyes narrowed and focused on my flushed face. That's My Desire by Frankie Laine was one of my favorite songs and being in his arms while listening to it was one of life's greatest pleasures.

We didn't stop dancing for close to two hours straight without taking any breaks. A portion of me was worn out, but there had never been a time when I felt so alive. My body temperature had increased because I was being held in his arms while we danced and because I could feel the movement of his muscles under my hands. I got goosebumps whenever he ran his fingertips down the back of my neck and shoulders.

I had fallen head over heels for Jacob. Even though I'd never experienced love before, I was sure that I loved him. What I intended to do about it, on the other hand, was a different matter. It wouldn't be long before my mother and father found out about us. In light of the fact that my father was extremely authoritarian, chaos would inevitably ensue. I forced the thoughts out of my head and made the decision that I would cross that bridge when it came to it.

It was getting late by the time we got back into town, so Jacob walked me back to the house, gave me a quick kiss goodbye, and told me that we would meet again on Tuesday.

March 18, 1947

The day I lost my heart . . .

THE PAST FOUR DAYS HAD BEEN SPENT WITH ME wistfully thinking about Jacob. He was required to work nights, but for some reason I had not questioned him about the nature of his work. I had no idea how or why that took place.

On the other hand, I would get to see him tonight.

When I finally left the house, it was five minutes before eight thirty as I snuck out through the kitchen.

I was running late. With a flashlight in hand, I quickly made my way to the beach.

As I rounded the bend, I caught a glimpse of Jacob up ahead. He saw me and started walking toward me. I picked up the pace and ended up running into him, wrapping my arms around his neck as he pressed his lips to mine while he cradled me close to his body. I felt safe and secure in his embrace.

"Being in your arms just seems to make everything better." I moved in closer to give him another kiss.

When it seemed like forever, he finally let go of me and took my hand, guiding me to a more secluded part of the beach. A couple of blankets had already been spread out on the ground by him. As soon as we were seated, he pulled me between his legs and kept one arm around my waist while we drank from a thermos of hot chocolate.

My heart beat faster whenever I was around him.

When I was with him, it was as if I'd known him my whole life, and when we're not together, I found myself yearning for his company with every fiber of my being. He made me feel safe and cherished, as if I could withstand anything that came my way.

To look at his face, I tilted my head ever-so-slightly to the side. "Will you tell me more about you?"

"What exactly do you want to know?" He gave me a friendly smile while gently stroking my face.

"Everything."

Then, with a chuckle, he pressed me against his chest and pulled me back. "I was born in the great state of New York, and I am twenty-two years old. In 1931, my parents made the move to Boston. Eleanor maintains her residence in Brookline, Massachusetts, where she also operates a respectable boarding house. Regularly, she comes to see me. The only time she was unable to come see me was when I was serving in the military in England, which was during the war."

I was concerned as I faced him. "Where specifically in England?"

"Leominster, located in the county of Hereford. Towards the end of the war, I was a member of the 5th Ranger Division. I seem to recall that the kids in the neighborhood were a lot of fun. In exchange for them buying us fish and chips, we used to give them candy and gum. Sometimes we even got free food! The children were the most enjoyable." The memory made him break out in a warm smile, and I was relieved to hear that he retained some positive experiences from the war.

I moved closer to him and gave him a kiss. "Thank you for sharing that with me."

My hair had become unclipped, so he took hold of it and smoothed it behind my ear while simultaneously massaging my face. He did this several times. "Now, I would like you to tell me about yourself." When I looked up into his eyes, I saw that they sparkled with desire... for me.

After giving me such a gentle kiss on the lips, he gave me the sweetest smile. "Just because you're sitting there looking stunning and ready to be kissed does not mean that I don't want to hear about you, Rose," he said. "I'm very interested in what you have to say."

I smiled back at him in response, before turning around and leaning against him. "Cape Elizabeth has been my home for the entirety of my life. Charlie was my older brother. During the war, he was shot and killed in France." I started to sniffle. When I thought about Charlie, I couldn't help but well up with tears every time.

"Rose, I beg you not to cry. Please. I am truly sorry to hear about the passing of your brother." Jacob gently wiped away my tears with the padded tips of his thumbs as I turned my head slightly to the side.

After a short while, I took a deep breath and wrapped my arms around Jacob's waist, drawing myself closer to the warmth of his body. "The other day, I brought up my younger brother, JT. It's the antics he pulls with his buddies Walt and Levi that never fail to make me laugh out loud. Father grounds him almost every other day. However, this does not last for very long because mother becomes irritated when he is constantly in the way throughout the day. After that, he will go and find his friends, which will result in him being grounded once more. He has the potential to be very obnoxious."

Jacob laughed. "Isn't that what it's supposed to be like when you have brothers?"

I gave him a light nudge in the side with my elbow. "Would you kindly assure me that Eleanor never found you to be an obnoxious brother?" I raised my eyebrow in question.

Jacob pulled me closer. "Most likely, but not always," he replied. "Eleanor is a great sister. Without her, I'm not sure where my life would have taken me."

I said, "I feel like that about JT—well, some of the time," just as Jacob leaned in to give me a sweet kiss. "I really don't want tonight to come to an end."

He looked at his watch as if the spell that had been

cast around us had been broken by my words. "It's getting late, there's a chance you'll be missed." Before we could untangle ourselves, Jacob took my hand and gave me a nod of approval. He picked me up off the ground and immediately carried me into his arms where we shared a passionate kiss.

After pulling away from the kiss, Jacob ran his fingers through my hair and tucked the ends behind my ears. "Will you meet me again, Rose? I'll be working the next few evenings, but I should be free to meet up with you on Friday."

"Friday it is." I couldn't help but laugh to myself as I began to count the seconds until then.

He exhaled a sigh as though he was sorry for the words that were about to follow. "Come on, I'll walk you back."

Jacob concealed the blankets by wrapping them in some type of water-resistant sheeting and placing them between some large rocks. After that, he grabbed hold of my hand and pulled me back into his arms before we begin our walk toward my residence. Before we came into view of Mother's parlor windows, he turned me toward him and kissed me with such fervor that he left me unable to take a breath. My toes curled and a tingly sensations ran through my skin, but before I knew it, he was pulling away once more. "I'll see you at the same place, but if you can make it earlier on Friday that would be great." Before turning on his heel, he leant over and kissed my knuckles. I just wanted to break down and cry about it.

How was it possible for me to feel this way for a man that I had only known for the past two weeks?

Chapter 8

I LOOK AT MY WATCH TO SEE IF I HAVE ENOUGH TIME to read some more, but I hadn't realized how much time had passed. I put down the diary and sit back, gazing far into the distance, across the sea.

My mind is racing with memories of Rose and Jacob, and I can't stop wondering what happened to them. I turn the pages of the diary, resisting the urge to turn to the back. This time, I promise myself that I will not skip ahead to the last entry. At the very least, I hoped not to do so. I wasn't exactly sure of my patience.

I gather my belongings and stroll back to the cottage to see if Thomas and Lucas had returned from their fishing trip.

It didn't take long for me to walk along the quiet beach path, and when I enter the cottage, I'm greeted by an eager Lucas.

"Auntie Mack, you've returned. Thomas caught two yellow perch and I caught one, so Thomas is gutting them. Will you prepare them for dinner?" Lucas inquires, his face lit up as he dances impatiently from foot to foot.

I approach him and kiss his cheek.

"Yuck, Auntie." He groans and rubs his face.

"How about me? I caught two, you know." Thomas says, winking at me and pointing to his cheek.

I walk over to Thomas, grinning, and place a kiss on his weathered cheek, enjoying his delight. "I appreciate you taking him fishing. He obviously had a great time."

"He did that. I certainly did as well. I don't think I've ever laughed so hard."

"He can have that effect on people. Come on, Thomas, show me how to cook this fish because I have no idea."

I quickly clean up the mess in the kitchen so I can start cooking, and when I turn around, Lucas is standing behind me. "I'd like to help you, Auntie Mack. You know, I caught one of them."

I ruffle his hair while laughing. "I think we both need to put on an apron because fish can be smelly."

"Yeah, it stinks in here." Lucas squeezes his nose.

The smell is really bad, so I open the windows and the kitchen door to try to get rid of it.

"I think we're ready now, Thomas."

"You're ready, but are the fish?" Thomas inquires.

Both Thomas and Lucas laugh like children.

"All right, guys, enough. At this rate, we'll never get any dinner."

DINNER HAD GONE WELL DESPITE THE FACT THAT I HAD a few extra hands in the kitchen, and the fish had been delicious with the seasoning Thomas had asked me to make. Lucas had also cleaned his plate, which surprised me because he had previously turned his nose up at fish.

"Auntie Mack?"

"What's up, Lucas?"

"Would you mind showing me some of the places Mommy and Daddy are going?"

I cast a glance at Lucas, who is dressed in his

favorite Power Rangers pajamas and holding his new children's atlas in the kitchen doorway.

He causes a lump to form in my throat. "I certainly will. Please come over here."

Lucas approaches and I lift him onto my lap as he places the book on the table.

"Let's go to France. If I recall correctly, they're supposed to arrive in Nice within the next few hours."

"I'll go find it."

I sit and watch him flip through the atlas, biting my tongue when he gets to the next page.

"Found it!"

I lean in close and kiss the top of his head. "Are you certain it's France and not South America?"

"Auntie Mack. Are you sure it's South America?" he complains.

"Well, then, you tell me what these letters are."

While Lucas tries to focus on them, I reach around him and point out the large letters that represent a country.

"B...R...A...Z...I...L." He looks at me, puzzled, as he begins to sound out the word. "Br...ah...Brazil. Ugh, gross. That's where you get your bananas."

Unable to help myself, I burst out laughing. "Let

me assist you in finding France. We might be here all night if I don't."

I flip back a few pages and point out the large country of France. Lucas pulls his first sticker from the back of the atlas and, with my help, locates Nice. I stare longingly at the sticker, hoping that one day I'll be able to visit, assuming I can get my head around a long flight.

"Let's tuck you into your bed."

Lucas leaps from my lap and dashes upstairs, leaving me behind with my usual hot chocolate and, of course, Rose's diary.

Chapter 9

March 19, 1947

I miss Jacob already . . .

IT HADN'T BEEN THAT LONG SINCE I'D SEEN JACOB. Actually, last night. I really missed him and wanted to talk to him about my day at work. I wanted his arms around me and, most importantly, his lips on mine. I'd been kissed before, but I'd never reacted to anyone like this before. I'd felt at ease with him...with his touch...since our first meeting. He listened to me as if he was interested in my ideas. He did not speak down to me or over me, but rather included me in the conversation. He looked at me as if I were the only other person on the planet.

I was in my room after a long day, unable to think of anything but the man who was tying my emotions in knots. A knock came on my door as I was about to change into something more comfortable. When I opened it, I found my mother on the other side, looking agitated. "Mother, what's wrong?"

"Oh, I'm fine, but Richard is downstairs, and he really wants to talk to you," she explained. Her excited smile made me nervous. I hoped she wasn't overjoyed because she thought wedding bells were on the way. That would never happen.

I clenched my teeth, a wave of obstinacy washing over me. "Please tell him I have a headache." I swooned onto my bed, placing my hand on my brow. I opened one eye to see my mother still standing in my room, hands on her hips, her smile gone, replaced by a dissatisfied frown.

"Put on your shoes and come on into the parlor. Now." She then shut the door.

Oh, fiddlesticks.

I went downstairs to the parlor wearing my scuffed-up shoes. Richard jumped up from his chair, nearly splattering his tea all over Mother as he went to put it down and raced toward me. He took my hands in his. "Rose, I've really missed you."

I didn't understand where he was coming from with this. I yanked my hands away from his. "Thank you for coming by Richard. How are you?"

"I'm all right. Thank you for inquiring." He took my elbow and led me over to the sofa, where he sat beside me.

When my mother stood up and excused herself, he poured me some tea.

He sagged in relief after my mother left. "What's gotten into you?" I inquired of him.

"This is a hot mess."

"What exactly is?" He was completely illogical to me.

He took a deep breath and dropped his head into his hands after a quick glance at me. "My father told me last night that if I didn't ask for your hand in marriage today, he would stop paying my allowance."

"Oh! Please don't tell me that's why you've come to see me. We've already talked about it."

"Then tell me no," he begged in despair.

I was stunned and whispered, "No."

He let out a sigh. "I apologize for everything, Rose. I truly am. Do you think we could still be friends?"

I was so relieved that this was over. "Yes, I would like that, but no talk about marriage."

"Thank you very much. "Would you like to go to the movies with me on Saturday?" he asked, smiling. "As friends," he quickly added.

Even though we were only friends, I hoped Jacob wouldn't mind if I went to the movies with another man. "That would be good."

"Then I'll pick you up at six-thirty. Is that all right?"

"Yes. I'll see you later." I let him out through the front door.

He stopped and grinned slightly as he was about to walk through it. "Um... Rose?"

I looked him in the eyes. "Yes."

"Your shoes have a tear in them."

I put my hand to my mouth, trying to hold back a burst of laughter, and shut the door behind him.

"What exactly did you say?"

When I turned around, Mother was standing behind me. I couldn't stop myself from staring at her. "I said no, and don't ask me again," I said adamantly.

"Well, Rose, really. How will your father react?"

"He's not the one who'd marry him," I retorted

dismissively. I dashed back up the stairs to my room, this time locking the door.

March 20, 1947

Only one more day . . .

I couldn't wait to see Jacob once more. I'd missed him so much, and even when I didn't see him, he took up so much of my time. Those thoughts had kept me going for the past few days.

After rejecting Richard's proposal, Father refused to speak to me, and Mother was even colder than usual. Father, in my opinion, was acting like a child.

"Achoo." The dust.

I'd been dusting the shelves and books in the library for two hours. I'd lost track of how many spiders I'd seen or how many times I'd sneezed.

Mr. Young decided he wasn't going to let us sit around doing nothing in the library today. That's why I was sneezing and covered in cobwebs.

"Boo."

Jayne was doubled over laughing when I turned around after jumping a mile.

"That wasn't very nice."

"It was amusing. You should look at yourself. You look a mess... " she trailed off.

"Thank you, and please keep quiet before Mr. Young finds us. What exactly are you doing here?" She rarely visited the library. My boss frightened her.

"Will you go on a double date with me tomorrow night?"

"Oh." I needed to think fast. "I'm sorry, Jayne, but I promised Mother I'd keep JT busy."

"You're seriously going to pass because of your brother?" she asked, stunned.

"I'm attempting to maintain peace after rejecting Richard. So, I am on this occasion." It was close to the truth, and I was desperate to keep the peace.

"I should get back to work. I'll see you later." She frowned and walked out of the library, waving over her shoulder as she went.

I ate dinner at home after a long day at work before taking JT to the beach. This time, we had a lot of fun looking for crabs. JT discovered two, while I discovered none. He gloated the entire way home, like a brat. I should stop calling him by his nickname, and maybe he'll act more mature.

JT was also known as Thomas James. He was twelve years old, and no matter what he thought, I adored him.

March 21, 1947

Tonight, I meet Jacob . . .

I TOLD MOTHER AND FATHER AT DINNER THAT I WAS going to town to meet some friends. I dashed up to my room and changed my clothes before they could respond.

I opened my closet and pulled out my new yellow dress, which had a low neckline and exposed too much of my breasts. It was daring, but I didn't care. Because I knew my mother would not approve, I wore a white cardigan over the dress and buttoned it up high. I slipped my feet into my yellow pumps and inspected my reflection in the mirror. I smiled, feeling good about how I looked.

When I opened the door to leave, I ran into JT. "What exactly are you doing lurking on the landing?"

"Are you going to meet him? That fella from the cliffs."

I was speechless and unsure what to say. "Um... What?" He gave me that look that said he knew he was going to get me in trouble. I opened my purse, pulling myself together. "Here." I gave him ten cents to buy a comic book. "You must keep quiet about who I'm meeting."

He was beaming from ear to ear. "Thanks, sis."

Brothers!

I crept down the backstairs and out the kitchen. I felt like I was floating through Mother's rose garden before doubling back toward the beach path.

Jacob was waiting for me as I rounded the bend. He saw me and smiled before beginning to walk toward me. It felt like coming home to be in his arms again. I drew back slightly, but Jacob's arms remained around my waist. Desire burned in his eyes as he looked down into mine. My skin began to tingle as I became more aware. I needed something, but I wasn't sure what it was.

He leaned in and grabbed my mouth with his. He

tasted of chocolate and felt fantastic. I didn't want to let him go.

All too soon, he broke from the kiss and placed small kisses all over my face. "I've really missed you, Rose."

"I've missed you, too."

He took my hand and led me to the shelter we'd shared the night before. He sat on the blanket and wrapped the other blanket around us both, keeping the evening chill at bay. I unbuttoned my cardigan without Jacob noticing, though he'd catch on soon enough.

"Please tell me more about yourself. I'm curious about everything," I said, and Jacob laughed.

"I currently work for the fire department, but my ambition is to become an engineer. I've applied for a job as an apprentice in Boston." He smiled. "I'm a huge baseball fan who can't wait for the season to begin. I'm a Boston Braves fan, and I'll be at the game against the Philadelphia Phillies on April 18th... Would you like to accompany me?"

"Yes. Will you take me with you to Boston if you get the job?" I waited for his response with bated breath.

He cupped his hands around my face. "Rose, I'll

take you anywhere you ask within my means." He
kissed me on the lips.

As he drew away, he noticed my chest and his eyes
nearly popped out of his head. I hid a smile as he
gulped. I was desperate to feel his hands on me. Heck.
I had no idea what was happening, but I was shiv-
ering all over. My skin felt alive, as if I were on fire.
The sensation was novel, but I craved more.

"Jacob, please kiss me." I spoke to him in hushed
tones.

He caressed my face with a trembling hand.
"Rose."

He sealed his lips to mine and sliding his tongue
into my mouth, he moaned in the back of his throat.
As my longing for Jacob grew stronger, I was
surprised by my own eager response to the touch of
his lips.

I climbed onto his lap and wrapped my arms
around his neck, trying to keep him close. One of his
hands traveled up my torso, leaving a trail of heat
over the top of my breasts.

With the pleasure more intense than I'd ever felt
before, I pulled my mouth away from the wet heat of
his. He kissed down my neck leaving me panting for
more as I arched into him, which brought me into

contact with the hardness between us. His lips continued to leave a blaze of fire across my chest and when he cupped one of my breasts, tingles centered between my legs.

He ran his fingers over one of my beaded nipples, which drew a loud gasp of surprise from between my lips. I had no idea that anything could feel so good. Jacob groaned as his lips moved between my breasts that weren't covered by my dress.

"Rose." He murmured. "My sweet Rose."

I couldn't stop rocking my hips on him, my body alive for the first time in my life.

His fingers rested on the first button on my dress as his eyes met mine. I knew what he silently asked and nodded my head. "Please... Yes... Please," I begged.

"Oh God, Rose." He unbuttoned the front of my dress and reached into my brassiere, baring my breasts to his eyes. My nipples were so hard that if it wasn't for the heated look on Jacob's face I'd have been embarrassed.

Jacob gently stroked over my aroused breasts and when he lightly pinched my nipples, I rubbed hard against his pelvis. I grasped hold of Jacob's shoulders and pushing myself harder against his groin, I heard his quick intake of breath. His head dipped toward my breasts where he suckled one into his mouth and used his hand to massage the other. My pleasure exploded in a downpour of fiery sensation. I saw fireworks...stars...rainbows. Oh, my goodness.

Panting, Jacob wrapped me up in his arms. "Heck... Rose. That was not supposed to happen."

"Can we do that again?" I laughed, feeling exhilarated.

He fastened my dress with unsteady hands and lifted me from his lap.

I felt rather languid after the pleasure he'd caused my body to experience.

Finally blushing, I glanced at Jacob and noticed the large bulge I'd been rubbing against.

He pulled his legs up with a wince and took some deep breaths. "We can do that again," he whispered.

After a few minutes, he stood and helped me up from the sand. "I need to get you home. That's not what I want to do with you, but I know it's what I *need* to do. Now. Before I lose further control with you," he said blushing. "I'm working until Wednesday. Do you want to go to the movies then?"

A twinge of guilt niggled at me as I remembered

my arrangement with Richard. Should I tell Jacob about my movie night with Richard?

We walked back to my house, hand in hand, and I decided I should. "Jacob. I'm going to the movies tomorrow with a friend, Richard." He stopped walking. "He really is only a friend. You're the one I want to be with."

"Okay." He turned and looked deeply into my eyes. "I can't say I like you going with another man, Rose, but I trust you."

He placed a goodbye kiss on my lips. We parted with the promise of the movies on Wednesday. In five days. It was difficult to put one step in front of the other when they only led away from him.

Chapter 10

I'm exhausted a week later. Lucas had been sick with a bad cold, which had kept both of us housebound, and then Thomas caught it. I insisted he move into Rose Cottage while he was sick so that I could care for him as well. Then, two days ago, I woke up in the middle of the night feeling yucky and sick, so Thomas took over as nursemaid because he was feeling better. Of course, Lucas tried to assist, but he kept getting in the way.

After missing the ocean for the past week, all I want is a walk on the beach. I've also missed Rose and Jacob because I've been too tired and then too sick to pick up the diary while playing Florence Nightingale.

I never expected to miss a story so completely, but I did. I'd hoped to enjoy Rose's writing.

Throwing off the covers, I climb out of bed and quickly dress in a pair of jeans, a T-shirt, and consider whether or not to wear a sweater, but after being sick, I decide one is required.

Standing in the doorway, I observe Thomas and Lucas interact. They appear to understand what the other wants without saying anything. It's sweet.

"You're awake, Auntie Mack. We're making you breakfast... You were supposed to eat it in your bed." Lucas doesn't seem impressed.

"Well, I'd love to eat your breakfast, but I'll sit here with you and Thomas. If that's okay with you? Then, after breakfast, we could go for a walk along the beach. I need to get some fresh air."

"Yeah!" Lucas yells as he sprints around the kitchen.

With the racket he's making, I have to put my hands over my ears.

"Lucas, please be quiet now. Your auntie is getting a headache from you." Much to my relief, Thomas' words manage to silence him.

They'd made my favorite pancakes, which I eat with a little butter and maple syrup. I happen to glance up as I put the first piece in my mouth and notice that both Thomas and Lucas are staring at me.

I pause in the middle of chewing.

"I dropped an eggshell into it." Lucas is beaming with delight.

"Oh."

Thomas begins to laugh as I continue to eat cautiously.

I clear my plate while only eating a few pieces of the shell. "That was delicious. Thank you very much."

"She really liked it." Lucas is overjoyed.

"Thomas, are you going to walk to the beach with us?" I ask as while clearing the breakfast dishes from the table.

"No, Mack, I don't think so. I'll accompany you all the way to my cottage."

Lucas's face sinks. "I don't want you to leave, Thomas. Are you unable to stay?"

Lucas is dragged onto Thomas' lap. "I'm only two minutes away. The problem is that I require my own space. I haven't lived with anyone in a long time, and while it's been nice staying here, I need to go home. I am grateful for everything you and your auntie have done for me. In fact, I'm sure your auntie will invite me to dinner if she feels like it."

"Think of yourself as invited. Now Lucas, you go and wash up and bring a sweater down with you. I don't want you to get sick again."

I turn to face Thomas and give him a good look. He appears pale, but in better health than he had been. "Are you sure you're feeling, okay?"

He laughs. "I'm perfectly fine. Tired. Unless I'm in my own bed, I don't sleep well."

"I understand what you mean. I'm a little like that, but for some reason, I've had no problems here. Perhaps it's the fresh air and proximity to the sea."

"Auntie Mack, I'm ready," Lucas announces as he enters the kitchen.

I turn to face Lucas, who is dressed appropriately in a sweater and sneakers.

"Come on, let's go. And no playing in the tidal pools today, Lucas. You've been ill."

"This isn't going to be any fun," he complains.

I smile and lead him out of the cottage before taking his hand in mine. We begin walking along the beach path with Thomas.

When we arrive at Thomas's cottage, I join him on the porch, while Lucas relaxes in the front lawn lounge chair.

"Thomas, may I ask you a question?"

"Go on."

"Are you, JT?"

Thomas abruptly stops what he's doing and sits down on the porch swing. "I haven't called myself that in a long time. It was her nickname for me, switching my initials around so no one would know she was talking about me," he explains as he wipes his brow with his hand. "Of course, it didn't take long for everyone to realize she was referring to me."

"Thomas, if talking about Rose is too painful for you, we can just leave it. I don't mean to cause you any problems," I express concern.

"She hated me," Thomas says quietly.

"Who?" I ask, surprised. "Rose?"

He gives a nod. "Yes, I was always trying to get her into trouble." He shakes his head.

"No, Thomas. You're mistaken. She wrote in her diary that she adores you. Wait a second." I quickly pull the diary from my purse and locate the relevant section. "This was written on March 20, 1947. 'JT is also known as Thomas James,' Rose says. He's twelve years old, and no matter what he thinks, I adored him.' Thomas, that's what she wrote in here."

"I never knew," he says, almost in tears.

He gets up and unlocks his front door after a few

moments of silence. "Don't worry, Mack. I'll be fine.
I'm glad you discovered her diary and informed me. It
means a lot to me." He attempts to reassure me. "You
go have fun with the boy, and I'll see you both later
for dinner."

Thomas shuts the door as I turn to face Lucas,
who is patiently waiting in the garden. I hope
Thomas is okay; after all, it must have been a shock to
discover his sister's words.

LUCAS AND I HAD BOTH NAPPED AFTER RETURNING
from the beach. Despite feeling better, the long walk
collecting clamshells and smooth bones had been
exhausting.

I am obsessed with shells and have them all over
my apartment. Lucas has painted some and stuck
them to some sort of clay item that he'd made for
my birthday for the past three years. I smile as I recall
the flowerpot, vase, and coffee mug he made for me.
They're all useless, but they mean more to me because
Lucas took the time to make them. I knew I'd cherish
them for the rest of my life.

After we've finished eating, Thomas decides to

stay while Lucas takes his bath so he can read him another Our Gang story before we go to bed.

I'm drinking coffee in the living room with Thomas and hoping he's decided to talk about Rose.

"What exactly do you want to know?"

"Tell me something about your sister."

"Oh, she was incredible. So full of life." He takes a deep breath and pauses. "I was with her the first time she met him. Does she write about it in her diary?"

"She does, indeed. You dragged her away from him, she claims."

As he recalls, Thomas laughs. "I did, indeed. Our father was a connoisseur. He would have made her life hell if he'd known she was interested in someone who wasn't wealthy. He barely allowed Rose to work at the library, but she refused to leave and stated that she needed to earn her own money. I don't think she enjoyed working there, but it was her chance to be free. It probably made her happy that she was going against Father's wishes."

He needs a minute. "I caught her sneaking off to meet him once or twice, so she could bribe me with ten cents to buy Our Gang comics. To keep me quiet, she went out and bought me the April 1st edition. It was our little secret because Father had told Mother I couldn't have that issue for misbehaving. I sometimes think that if I had told my father about what she was doing, she might still be alive."

I look at him, wondering if I heard him correctly. "What exactly do you mean?"

Thomas returns my gaze with a glance out the window. "She died on April 14, 1947, the night she was fleeing with him. She'd gone to meet him, to marry him, I suppose. That was my last encounter with her." Thomas wipes away his tears.

"How did she die?" I inquire.

"That's something I really don't want to talk about."

"Do you happen to know if she met up with Jacob?" I can't stop asking questions.

"No, she didn't make it. I overheard my father talking to my mother a few days later. It turned out to be about Jacob. I overheard him telling her that Jacob had called the house and asked for Rose. He informed Jacob that she'd married Richard. He stated that Jacob sounded very upset and then hung up on him."

"Oh my, so if he's still alive, all this time Jacob thinks Rose changed her mind and didn't love him," I cry. "That's so heartbreaking, Thomas. I need to contact him and tell him what happened to Rose."

"If he is still alive, he will be older than I am. When I overheard my parents talking, my father mentioned that he was three years older than Rose and thus..." Thomas's voice trailed off as he calculated, "around ninety, I think."

"I have to give it a shot, Thomas. You can see and feel how much she loved him if you read her diary, and if his feelings were the same as hers, he has to know." I still have tears streaming down my cheeks. "If he is still alive and remembers her, which I believe he will, he has the right to know the truth."

"I think you're right." He is getting ready to leave.

"Thank you for sharing that with me, Thomas. Knowing how their love ended breaks my heart."

"You have a tender heart," Thomas says as he kisses my cheek.

"Will you be okay walking home? It's completely dark out there."

"I've been walking home in the dark since I was five years old," he chuckles as he walks out the door.

"Then good night. Why don't you come to breakfast with us? Pancakes, eggs, and sausage," I offer as an enticement.

"I'll be right there at eight."

"Goodnight."

I stand on the doorstep, watching Thomas walk home. Rose and Jacob occupy my thoughts; their story is heartbreaking.

I lock up the cottage for the night and go upstairs to shower and change into my pajamas.

Back downstairs, I prepare my usual hot chocolate and pull Rose's diary from my purse before retiring to bed with a heavy heart. Knowing how it all ends brings tears to my eyes, but Rose's story is so bittersweet that I can't put it down.

Chapter 11

March 22, 1947

Movie night with Richard . . .

RICHARD ARRIVED IN HIS FATHER'S CAR, AS PROMISED, calling for me. I was looking forward to seeing the film Blue Skies. Bing Crosby was a favorite of mine. I couldn't bring myself to tell Richard that I'd already seen the movie with Jayne. At the very least, it was a fun movie to watch, so I didn't mind seeing it twice.

We took our seats, and Richard was ever the gentleman, despite the fact that I had reminded him it wasn't a date and we were just friends.

"Rose, are you comfortable?" he asked quietly. The movie theater was packed tonight.

"I'm fine, thank you. Do you like Joan Caulfield? I think she's fantastic."

"She's fine, but I prefer Bing Crosby. I believe he is very good."

The movie began to play, and the chitchat came to a halt. I was actually relieved. I had no idea what to say to him.

During the break, I went to the restroom and was about to open the door when I was grabbed by two hands. I was dragged into the cloakroom before I could even comprehend what was going on. Jacob.

"What—"

He pressed his lips against mine, thrusting his tongue between my lips. I clung to him, moaning.

"Rose. I can't get you out of my mind." As my hands curled around his neck, he kissed me again. His arms wrapped tightly around my waist, keeping me close to his body, and the hardness at his pelvis.

"I just wanted to remind you of who your guy is."

"Okay," I agreed, grabbing his hair, and yanking him back down to me, unable to get enough of the man.

When the bell rang to alert everyone that the movie was about to resume, we both exhaled heavily.

"I've got to get back to work. One of the guys is pitching in for me." He stroked my cheek.

"I should return as well. I'm going to miss you terribly." I had to fight back the tears.

"I'll miss you too, Rose. I'll see you later. Now go."

He pushed me through the curtains after a quick kiss on the lips. I quickly returned to Richard, who looked at me with wide eyes. Oh, heck.

"Do you have a cold or something? You appear to be very flushed."

"I think I might be, but I'm fine." I sat down again, trying not to look at him until I felt his hand creep across the back of my chair. "What exactly are you doing?"

"Um, I'm stretching." I couldn't decide whether to believe him or not.

"Well, then, stretch somewhere else."

He huffed and lowered his arms.

After the intermission with Jacob, the film seemed to drag. The lights eventually came on, and everyone stood up to stretch their legs before leaving.

"Would you like to go have a slice of pie and some

chocolate milk?" My stomach grumbled as I was about to refuse. "I'll take that as a yes."

I didn't have much of a choice, so I let Richard drive me to the diner. He began to lead me to the back when he froze and returned to the booths at the front of the room.

"Richard, who are they?" He appeared to be attempting to avoid the three men seated near one of the windows.

"I honestly don't know."

He was grumpy now, and I was hesitant to say he appeared troubled. "Richard... "

"Please don't bother asking again, Rose."

"Okay." That was strange.

We ate in silence, but by the time we were done, and he was driving me home, he seemed to have recovered.

"Thank you for this evening, Rose. Maybe we'll do it again someday?"

I tried to keep my yawn hidden. "Maybe," I muttered behind my hand as he led me to the front door. He made me nervous because I assumed he was expecting a goodnight kiss, but JT opened the door and saved the day.

I said goodnight quickly and dragged JT inside, closing the door behind us.

March 24, 1947

Richard doesn't have to marry me . . .

IT'D BEEN TWO DAYS SINCE I'D SEEN JACOB. I REALLY missed him. I was sitting on the porch, daydreaming about the beach night, when Richard drove up in his father's car.

He climbed out and dashed over to me. "Would you like to go for a drive with me, Rose?"

I was unsure.

"Please?"

Oh well, what the heck. I wasn't doing anything in particular. "OK, fine. Let me get my jacket and purse."

I dashed inside, grabbed what I needed, and dashed back outside. Richard flung open the door for me. While Richard shut the door and ran around to the other side, I climbed into his father's luxurious car and admired the cream leather interior with a dark mahogany wooden dashboard.

"Richard, what's going on?" I was both nervous and fascinated.

"My father has agreed that I am not required to marry you. So, I thought we could celebrate with pie and chocolate milk," he replied, a childlike grin on his face.

I burst out laughing. "All right, then, let's celebrate."

He drove into town and parked in front of a crowded diner. As we entered, I noticed Jayne, who had just finished her meal. I approached her and sat down beside her.

"Are you here alone?" Jayne took a look around.

"Richard wants to celebrate the fact that he is not being forced to marry me."

I laughed because her eyes nearly popped out of her head.

"Rose, Sandy is on her way over with our favorite pie and milk." Richard said. "Hello there, Jayne. Would you like something?"

"No, I've had enough... Thank you, however." She gave a polite smile.

Richard sat across from me and struck up a

conversation with Jayne. I wished for a few quiet moments alone with Jayne as they talked. I wanted to tell Jayne about Jacob, but I was afraid she would tell someone else. She was my best friend, but she struggled, a lot, with keeping things to herself.

I had just finished my pie when I noticed JT sitting at the back of the diner with Levi, Walt, and some girls.

Excusing myself, I approached their table. JT turned bright red and stood up when he saw me. He grabbed my arm and pulled me away from his friends, out of their hearing range.

"What exactly are you doing here, sis?"

"I'm in the company of Jayne and Richard. So, how about you? You know you're not allowed in here."

"I'm with Walt and Levi." He cast a glance in their direction.

"I've got eyes, JT... I'll accompany you back, so you don't get in trouble with Father."

He burst out laughing. "Wouldn't want that, sis." He returned to his friends, said his goodbyes, and then returned to me.

"Let me tell Jayne and Richard I'm leaving," I said as I quickly crossed the room to where they were sitting.

"Sorry, but I'm going to walk back to the house with JT before Father gets home."

"Please don't leave, Rose. Can't JT just walk back?" Richard whined, frowning at JT, who had stuck his tongue out at him.

I pushed him away. "Stop doing that, it's bad manners." I returned my attention to Jayne and Richard. "I really need to make sure he arrives without causing any further problems. I'll catch up with you both later." I turned quickly and grabbed JT's arm, dragging him out of the diner.

March 26, 1947

The night I became a woman . . .

JT HAD CAUGHT ME SNEAKING OUT OF THE HOUSE YET again. I owed him an issue of Our Gang. He was extracting a lot from me.

Jacob awaited me at the bottom of the driveway. I jumped into his arms, and we kissed and kissed as he spun me around. "I've missed you so much." He stroked my cheek. "My Rose."

"Always."

"Let's go, before we miss the bus." As we walked to the bus stop, he took my hand in his. We needed to be more cautious because I didn't want Father to find out that I was seeing someone other than Richard. But I didn't mind so much when Jacob was clutching me.

We were going to see Betty Grable in The Shocking Miss Pilgrim. I had seen her previous films and was excited to see this one. Going with Jacob only improved things.

Jacob held my hand the entire way there, and I cuddled into him during the movie, moving in slightly to give him a quick kiss.

We only had time to catch the bus home after the movie, so we jumped off a stop early. We walked along the cliffs toward my house to spend some extra time together. Jacob had his arm around my shoulders, and mine was tightly wrapped around his waist. He felt incredible, and I didn't want to let go.

Jacob abruptly turned around, cupped my face in his hands, and caressed my cheeks with his thumbs. "Rose, I love you," he said quietly.

I extended my hand to him and tangled my fingers in the hair at the nape of his neck. He shivered, his own lips covering mine. I searched for his tongue while moaning, and the gentle massage sent currents of desire racing through my body.

I moved closer, breathing heavily, and when he placed his hands on my waist, he guided me snug against him.

I gasped for breath, pulling my willing mouth away from his demanding one, and whispered, "Make love to me, Jacob." He appeared startled but quickly recovered.

"Are you sure?" he asked me seductively, moving my hair behind my ears with an unsteady hand.

"More now than ever." I kissed the back of his hand.

"We're way too far away from my apartment." He appeared distressed.

"Then let's go to the beach. It's late, and no one will be around. It's also dark and secluded."

He sighed. "Rose."

I took his hand in mine and began to lead him toward the beach, but after only a few steps, he picked me up and carried me the rest of the way.

We stood facing each other after he'd retrieved the

hidden blankets and laid them on the sand before he smiled and began removing his clothing. His blazer was first, then his shirt and tie. I unbuttoned the front of my dress and let it fall down my body, kicking it to the side. That was followed by my slip. I stared at the beautiful man as we stood in our underwear. He had broad shoulders, a muscular chest, and a trim waist, with only a smattering of hair on his stomach that slid down into his shorts.

He drew me close by taking my unsteady hand in his. I smoothed my palms over his skin and placed my hand on his naked chest. He was stunning. I looked up, searching for his eyes in the starlight as I dealt with the upheaval in my emotions.

Knowing this was the man I loved gave me the confidence to pursue my desires. Leaning in, I kissed his chest, then his nipples, only to hear him groan, which encouraged me to keep going.

He pushed us both onto the blanket, gently easing me down before crushing me to him and reclaiming my lips with such passion that my entire body began to throb.

As he leaned over me, he unhooked and removed my brassiere, inhaling sharply in delight. He finally moved and kissed my taut nipples, rousing a melting sweetness within me as he placed kisses all around my breasts.

He continued his heated kisses on my skin, taking hold of my panties with his fingers before looking up, as if asking permission.

"Yes... I'm yours, Jacob... So yes."

He dragged them down my legs and away, followed by his shorts. He stared at me while kneeling between my thighs. "You're so beautiful, Rose." His voice was hoarse.

I couldn't believe how tingly and overheated I felt. I was still not nervous, only excited. "Beautiful...and, so big."

He chuckled, and I realized I'd said something out loud. I blushed but kept my gaze fixed on his tense body.

Jacob groaned as his hands began to explore my thighs, and then his lips teased a tight dusky pink nipple as he moved up. He paused to kiss me, whispering loving words.

Gathered against his warm body as he half lay over me, I felt his arousal nudging my inner thigh— hot and pulsing with his need.

One hand slid down my quivering stomach to the swell of my hips before I gasped as he stroked my curls with his fingers. When he dipped his finger inside of me, his breath became more ragged. "Rose, I really need you."

"Love me, Jacob."

His eyes were red-hot.

He closed his eyes, breathed deeply, and guided his flesh to where we both needed him to be.

My body resisted the intrusion at first, but with some delightful coaxing from Jacob's mouth and hands, he was all the way inside of me.

When he held still, his face twisted in pain, so I traced his lips with my finger and moved slowly down toward his chest to rub his hardened nipples.

He shivered. "I need to move."

"Yes... Move," I pleaded.

That was all it took for him to make love with me on our beach, as the night encircled our warm bodies and the waves crashed against the rocks in the distance.

As a moan of ecstasy slipped through my lips, I was held on the periphery, knowing that something exquisite awaited me when I crossed the threshold.

The sensation of him swelling inside me struck a deep chord, and when I gasped for air, Jacob grunted my name and shuddered in my arms. My body yielded to the searing need that had been building, and when I vibrated with liquid fire, Jacob held me until the storm passed.

He took a deep breath and slowly slipped out of my body, making me shiver. When he drew me back into his arms, the cold air kissing my burning skin, I felt so relaxed and satiated.

"Are you all right, Rose?"

"Oh, yes." I smiled and gently kissed his lips.

Jacob reached for his shorts and wiped himself before turning to face me. "Let me look after you."

I did what he asked and watched while he cleaned me up. He tossed his shorts to the side and laid down beside me, but I was feeling brave and wanted to look at him, having never seen a naked man before. I sat down and began to caress him with my eyes. My gaze shifted from his face to his chest to his hips... I flushed and looked up at him quickly. As he watched me, his eyes narrowed, and his breathing became labored.

When I looked at him again, his flesh twitched and swelled before my eyes.

"Rose, please stop staring at me. We won't be able to do it again tonight. It will be far too painful for you."

I didn't listen and reached out to touch him,

surprised by how hot and smooth he felt, though I couldn't stop myself from smiling as he throbbed against my palm.

I rubbed his flared crown, smiling, as he arched his hips up from the sand and a husky plea fell from his lips.

"Jacob, please make love to me once more before I have to go home."

He groaned and pulled me down under him, sliding inside of me and telling me how much he loved me. He kissed my lips gently and made love to me again, promising to see me again soon.

Chapter 12

IT'S BRIGHT AND EARLY WHEN THOMAS ARRIVES bearing a gift of daisies, which he shoves at me with a slight blush. "Picked you these on the way."

Smiling, I take the flowers and give him a kiss on his weathered cheek. "Thank you, Thomas. I don't ever remember being given flowers by a gentleman before." I stretch up to the top shelf of the cupboard for a vase.

"That guy in that fancy suit at your apartment gave you flowers," Lucas states, having overheard.

"Yes, but he wasn't a gentleman. Now go wash up and stop listening to adult conversations." I try to hide my embarrassment by setting the table for breakfast.

Sometimes I really wished I could gag Lucas. He's my nephew and I love him, but sometimes... *Ugh!*

I watch Thomas who appears to still be chuckling at Lucas's comment. "Are you all right, Thomas?" I ask. I take in his appearance, and he seems better this morning but that hadn't stopped me from worrying about him last night.

"I'm fine. Don't be worrying about me."

I give him a long look. "I won't...for now."

"I was wondering if Lucas would like to come back with me to look through some more comics."

"That would be fine. What comics are they?"

No sooner has Thomas sat at the table, then I place his breakfast in front of him. "Thanks, Mack. *Our Gang.* I have every issue as well."

I sit at the table now that Lucas has joined us. "You know I've heard of them. They're the 'Little Rascals' characters, right?"

"That's right. I have the first issue in October 1942, to the last one before they added Tom and Jerry, which would be issue thirty-eight in November 1947. I didn't care much for the *Tom and Jerry* stories," he says, enjoying his breakfast.

"Wow, that's some collection you must have."

"I know."

We finish the rest of our breakfast in silence, apart from Lucas, who keeps slurping his milk. Once finished he tracks his parents travels throughout the atlas with Thomas.

Not long after, the two head out, hand in hand. I'm surprised with how quickly they have become friends. Lucas is used to spending time with older people, because of his grandparents and where they live, but it usually takes a lot longer for him to warm up to someone new. Then again, Thomas isn't like the people at my parents' village. He's, different—all grumpy and lovable on the outside, and like a mischievous little boy on the inside, so perfect for Lucas.

"THOMAS?" LUCAS SAID WITH A QUIZZICAL LOOK ON HIS face. "Why don't you like Tom and Jerry?"

Thomas hadn't expected that question and burst out laughing. "I preferred the *Our Gang* kids. They used to get into trouble like I did as a child." He grinned. "Used to give me some good ideas, too."

As they walked hand in hand to Thomas's cottage, it brought back memories of another time. Except he was the child, and his sister, Rose, was the one holding his hand. She had been taking him to the beach, probably close to seventy-five years ago now, when he was five or six.

Once he opened his cottage door, Lucas ran inside, straight to the living room where Thomas kept the comics for him to read. Thomas followed behind him at a slower pace with his mind still on Rose. He hadn't thought about her in a long time. He'd loved his sister, and always thought she'd died hating him until Mack had started to read the diary.

He'd lived with regret about that final night, and in seventy years, he hadn't spoken about it. If only he'd told his father, perhaps Rose would have lived her life with the man she'd obviously loved. It wouldn't have been easy at first because of their fathers strictness, but if their love were true, they would have made it work.

An excited Lucas brought him back to the present. "Can I look at this one, Thomas, please?"

He glanced down. "Not that one." He removed it from Lucas's excited fingers as he pulled out the next issue and offered it to him. "Try this one."

Thomas moved away from Lucas and walked the short distance to his bedroom. He felt so old. The comic in his hands, as he glanced down at it, brought back the memories as though they had happened only yesterday. Sitting on the side of his bed, he placed the comic on his night table to read later, when he was alone.

It was dated April 1, 1947, the comic his sister had bought him as a surprise. She'd left it on his bed the night she'd died. He'd placed it into the box with the other issues, having never opened it.

Perhaps it was time to lay old ghosts to rest and read it.

I NOW HAVE THE MORNING ALONE, SO I DECIDE TO retrieve my laptop. I really need to try and find Jacob. Heck, I'm half in love with him myself.

I know his name is Jacob Evans, and going with his age, he was born around 1924 or 1925. I decide to check Boston first and start to get all excited when only one result appears for a man named Jacob Evans in 1924. As I look at the information, I'm delighted there is no death certificate, at least in the state of Massachusetts, but there is a marriage license for a Jacob Evans dated April 19, 1947. Unfortunately, after I purchase credits to view the license, a message pops up saying, that due to a fire there is no copy on file. I pause and tap my lip in thought as I ponder the date. Is this the same man that Rose loved? Why would he get married so quickly? Still, I have no other leads so I continue following the trail of this Jacob Evans.

After about ten minutes, I find a telephone number and address for him in Brookline, Boston. I'm not sure whether to get in touch or not as he appears to get married a week after Rose died. I find it strange, even if he'd spoken to Rose's parents by then.

With a deep breath, I pick my phone up and dial the number, which is answered on the second ring.

"Evans' residence," a feminine voice answers.

"Oh, hello. My name is Mackenzie Harper, and I was wondering if this is the correct number for a Mr. Jacob Evans?"

"What's the reason for the inquiry?"

"Whom I speaking to, please?" I ask in reply. I need to be a bit cautious in case I'm talking to his wife.

"I'm Martha, Mr. Evans housekeeper." Then she

goes silent, having realized she's practically admitted to me that I have the correct Jacob.

"All right, Martha, this is going to sound strange, but I've come across a diary dated March and April 1947. It contains information about a Jacob Evans. If your employer is the same Jacob Evans who lived in Cape Elizabeth, Maine, during that time, then I really need to speak to him. I'm concerned he's been living all this time thinking something happened that didn't. If that makes any sense?"

"That's some story, Miss Harper. I'll have to find out for you. Can I take your number and your address?"

I give her the phone number and address for Rose Cottage, and express again, how urgent the matter is. I really hope Martha passes the message on. Otherwise, I'll have to visit once Lucas has gone home to his parents.

"I have it. Thank you." Then Martha hangs up.

"Who was that, Martha?"

Martha quickly turned with an audible gasp of surprise. "Oh, Mr. Dean. I didn't know you were home. It was a young lady inquiring about your grandfather."

Dean placed his motorcycle helmet on top of the side table. "What about my grandfather?"

Martha was flustered. "She said she'd discovered a diary from 1947 and wanted to know if the Jacob mentioned was your grandfather. It can't be, really, because apart from the war, I don't think he lived anywhere other than here, and certainly not Maine."

"Hmm, did you take her contact details?"

He walked over to Martha and took the information from her. "Please don't mention anything until I've had time to check this out."

"If you're sure, Mr. Dean?"

"I am."

Dean had been thinking about escaping for a while now, and as he glanced down at the information on the piece of paper, he rubbed his fingers over the address. He needed to get away from his mother, who kept throwing Cynthia at him and going on and on about getting married. All because she wanted grandchildren. She really was driving him nuts, and with the perfect excuse to disappear for a short while, he wasn't about to pass it up.

Escaping to his room, he tossed his jacket onto

the bed and dropped his large frame into the chair at his desk. Opening the lid to his laptop, Dean brought up a search engine and had a look at available summer rentals near Cape Elizabeth. He smiled when he saw his luck was holding—there was a cottage right next door to the mystery caller's address, and it appeared to be available for the next few weeks.

After he'd debated with himself about whether this really was a good idea or not, he picked up his phone and dialed the contact number before he could change his mind.

His last contract had ended, and the new graphic work he had scheduled didn't start for another two months so it was the perfect time to head out on vacation.

He paid the deposit with his credit card and arranged to pay the rest in cash when he collected the keys from his new landlady.

On his way out of the house, Dean left a message with Martha for his mother, saying he had gone away for a few weeks, much to Martha's amusement. She knew he would do anything to avoid his mother and her matchmaking.

Dean climbed onto his Harley and headed north

up the coast, thinking about the mysterious Miss
Mackenzie Harper.

MID-AFTERNOON SOON ARRIVES WHEN I HEAR MY
phone ring and dash to answer it, only to find my
sister Melinda on the other end.

"Hi sis, how's everything? Is Lucas, okay? Any
gorgeous guys? Bored yet?"

I sigh in relief when Melinda finally shuts up to
catch a breath. For some reason, when Melinda is on
the phone, I can hardly shut her up, but talking to her
in person, she can hold a perfect conversation.
"Everything's okay. Lucas is great. No gorgeous guys,
unless you count a charming elderly man named
Thomas, and no, we're not bored yet."

"Sorry, Mack." Melinda giggles down the phone as
she realizes she hasn't shut up long enough for me to
answer her questions.

"It's all right. I'm used to you by now."

While I'm listening to my sister chat away, I hear a
motorcycle outside. I plaster my nose up against the
kitchen window in time to see a jean-and-leather clad

guy pull up next door. He looks a fine specimen—tall, dark, and mysterious.

I grab a magazine off the counter and use it to fan myself because I've started to get all hot and bothered. He looks delicious, and I really hope that when he removes his helmet, his face matches the rest of him.

"Mack, are you listening to me?" Melinda asks.

"Yes."

"No, you're not. And did I hear a motorcycle?"

"Yes, you did, and a very hot guy has just pulled up outside next door. Hope he's moving in. He looks sinful." I laugh at my sister. For once, I've managed to shut her up. I turn around to find Lucas standing behind me with a big grin on his face. "Here, talk to your mother." I pass him the phone.

I continue to gaze at the guy next door and have tuned out the conversation Lucas is having with his mother about Thomas.

Biker guy has removed his helmet. He's tanned, has plenty of muscles, and cropped dark hair. Mouthwatering.

Mmm, I won't mind getting to know him. Things are looking up for this vacation.

Chapter 13

March 27, 1947

We embrace in the library . . .

WHEN I WOKE UP THIS MORNING, I WAS MORE IN LOVE than ever with Jacob. He said that he wanted to become an engineer and there were opportunities in Boston. I really hoped he would take me with him when he left. He said he would take me anywhere I wanted to go but the only place I wanted to be was with him. He also told me that he really loved me. He made me feel so special.

I bumped into Jayne on the way to work, she was

dashing to the office where she worked. Late again. "Jayne, if you didn't spend so much time getting ready, you wouldn't be late so often," I pointed out.

"I have to look perfect, Rose. Perfection takes time."

I rolled my eyes and laughed.

"Come on. If you're going to walk with me, you need to speed up some," Jayne said.

Well, there went my leisurely walk.

We dashed through town when Jayne started giving me odd looks. I had to know why so I pulled her to a stop. "What's wrong?" *Was she blushing?* "Jayne?"

"Richard has asked me out to dinner," she blurted.

For a second, I stared at her, and then started to laugh in relief. She didn't seem too impressed with my giggling. "I'm glad he's moving on. He's a nice guy, but not for me."

She stood with her hands on her hips. "Are you seeing that man from the tearoom?"

Heck. "You do realize you're close to being very late for work." I blurted trying to deflect her question.

"Oh, no. I'll see you later." She panicked.

Lucky escape.

I finally arrived at work and was greeted by Mr.

Young. He was in a tizzy because two of the staff hadn't shown up for work. There were about six people already in the library, which was unusual so early in the morning so I could understand his stress.

I followed him to the staff room and stashed my jacket and purse, then turned around and practically bumped into him. "Mr. Young, please calm down," I told him, safe in the fact that he wouldn't fire me today since I was the only one there.

"Rose, there are a lot of people out there this morning and only you here to help them. What are we going to do?"

What an idiot.

"Mr. Young. I'm quite capable of helping whoever needs help. There aren't that many people in there."

We walked out to the main library floor, and I headed over to the front desk to check some books out for four of the people. "Mr. Young, I'm going to place these books back on the shelves. Are you capable of looking after the remaining two?" I asked, getting the evil look from him.

He ushered me away with his hands. I quickly grabbed the books that needed to be returned to the shelves and headed to the geography section first, then, with the last remaining book, the history section.

As I'd placed the last book on the shelf, I heard a throat being cleared behind me. I turned, delighted to discover that it was Jacob. I quickly glanced around to make sure there was no one close before I took his hand and pulled him into the storage closet next to where he was standing.

"Are you all right?" he asked, caressing my face.

I gave him a radiant smile. "Oh, Jacob. I am more than all right. Please kiss me."

He placed small kisses over my eyes, nose, and cheeks before sealing his mouth to mine in a beautiful kiss.

"I really want to go to Boston with you," I confessed. "I love you and want to be with you all the time."

"Your parents wouldn't let you come away with me, and you know that."

I grinned. "I'm not planning on telling them. I'm going to sneak away with you."

"Now, Rose. I really don't think that's a good idea."

"Don't worry, it will be fine, and probably after a week or two, they'll forget all about me." I realized what I'd said was more than likely the truth. It caused me to frown sadly for a moment, but that sadness was chased away when I took in Jacob's beautiful face.

"I'll try and pop in again one day soon. I'm on nights for now and won't be able to meet you, but I had better go before I get you into trouble. This conversation isn't over." He kissed me quickly before I could argue with him.

We both slipped out of the closet, and I stood watching Jacob walk away as Mr. Young walked around the corner, heading in my direction.

"Rose, I've been looking for you. Where have you been?" he asked, looking back and forth between me and Jacob's departing form.

"I've been placing books back on the shelves like I said." I walked toward the desk and tried not to laugh at Mr. Young, who was huffing and puffing after me.

March 28, 1947
Why me . . .

I was walking along the cliffs with Richard, who seemed to have developed a nervous twitch. "Richard, is something wrong?"

He took a deep breath. "Rose, I have to ask your father's permission to marry you."

I was stunned and stared at him. Not this again. I really thought this had all ended.

"My father has been talking to yours, which has set this whole thing off again." He paused and held my shocked gaze. "Rose? You know I'm awfully fond of you and I know that you are fond of me. We may grow to love each other." He offered a wry smile.

I sat down rather heavily on a large rock and looked at him, not knowing what to say. Richard crouched down in front of me, taking my hands into his. I was still in shock and left them there.

"Richard, I can't marry you. I'm sorry our parents are putting you in this position, but please, don't ask my father for my hand. My life will be unbearable at home if you do."

He sighed heavily. "I'll tell my father something to put him off for a short while, but Rose, you're actually the only woman I would consider marrying."

I looked quickly into his eyes. "I don't know what

to say. I thought you were all right with us just being friends?"

"I am, but for my father pushing me, I wouldn't be here talking to you about this." He let go of my hands and sat beside me. "Being friends makes the decision easier for me...at least we would have that friendship in our marriage—many don't even have that. I will have to ask your father eventually, Rose. I have to."

"I need to go back." I turned and began walking back to the house rather quickly with tears pouring down my face.

It wasn't as though I could admit that I was in love with Jacob. My father would hit the roof. What the heck was wrong with Father?

April 1, 1947

   I really miss Jacob . . .

I REALLY MISSED TALKING TO JACOB AND BEING WITH him so imagine my delight when I spotted him walking into the library. I looked around to make sure Mr. Young wasn't present. Then I followed him to the history section.

He looked really tired. I took one look at him, grasped his hand, and pulled him to a dark corner. I took his weary face into my hands and pulled him down to meet my lips. "I love you."

"I've missed you so much." He rested his forehead against mine and looked into my eyes. "Oh, Rose, I love you."

Still holding his face, I used my fingers to brush the hair out of his eyes. He turned his head and kissed my palm.

"I still don't know when I'm free to meet you, but I'll let you know as soon as I have a free night." He ran his hand over his face. "I'm so tired. I need to catch up on some sleep." He quickly kissed me and with one long, lingering look, he walked out of the library.

April 4, 1947

Finally, I get to meet Jacob again . . .

I WAS UP IN MY ROOM BRUSHING MY HAIR, READY TO GO and meet Jacob. He'd come into the library last night just before it had closed, and after a rather hot embrace in the store cupboard, he'd asked me to meet him behind the library tonight. My mind was whirring with thoughts of him, thoughts of leaving with Jacob for Boston.

"Rose?" my father shouted from downstairs.

I threw my brush back onto the dressing table and ran out of my room. I hurried down the stairs, wondering what Father wanted. It was very rare for him to call me down as he didn't really take much interest in me, unless it concerned marrying me off to Richard.

When I walked into the front parlor, Richard was sitting there with an odd smile on his face.

Upon seeing me, he stood and walked over, taking my hand into his. I had a really bad feeling about this. I tried to pull my hand free, but he tightened his hold, so I stamped on his foot.

"Rose," my father roared, "that is not the behavior of a young lady, especially toward her fiancé."

I froze. *What did he say?*

My father saw the shock on my face. "Richard has asked for your hand in marriage, and I have agreed."

I looked at my mother, who refused to meet my gaze. Richard looked as though he wanted to be elsewhere, and Father looked...relieved.

My tears were ready to fall. "So, you finally found a way to get rid of me." Anger flared in my eyes and matched the anger in my fathers. "There is no way I am going to marry Richard." I turned to him. "I'm sorry Richard, but I can't." I whirled toward Father. "I will only marry for love and Richard is a friend, and that is all he ever will be."

I turned and ran out of the house in tears. Richard called out. I ignored him.

With tears running down my face, I ran to the library and hoped Jacob was already waiting for me. I really needed his arms around me.

Jacob saw me coming from around the corner and began walking toward me. I ran straight into his arms and held on tightly as I cried all over him.

"Rose, what's wrong? What's happened?"

"Richard asked my father if he could marry me, and Father said yes." Jacob stilled at my announcement. "I told Father there was no way I was marrying him or anyone that I don't love. I had to get away, so I ran straight here."

Jacob placed a tender kiss to my lips, before he asked, "Do you want to go to my apartment?"

I nodded, and by the time we arrived at his apartment my tears had dried up, but I was left feeling angry that my parents had betrayed me. Leading the way inside, Jacob glanced around, nervously.

The apartment was small but nice and clean. The living room had a kitchen attached with a separate eating area. There were two doors off from the hall, which I presumed led to a bathroom and bedroom.

Jacob led me directly to the bathroom to wash my face. Afterwards, I felt ten times better and went looking for him.

I found him in the kitchen, warming some milk. I stood and watched him. He was gorgeous. My heart thumped in my chest. It felt so right being together in his apartment.

He turned and caught me watching him. His whole face lit up. "Are you feeling better?" He walked over and took my face between his palms. He pulled me closer and placed a gentle kiss on my waiting lips.

I wrapped myself around him and held on. After a few minutes, I looked up into his eyes. "Make love to me, Jacob. Show me how much you love me."

He stared at me for the longest time, then took me by the hand and led me to his bedroom. He stood in front of me, and my heart pounded when he started unbuttoning my dress. Reaching out, I made quick work of unbuttoning his shirt and sighed when I felt the smooth skin of his naked chest beneath my fingers. Groaning, Jacob leaned closer and captured my lips in a hungry kiss, causing goosebumps to erupt all over my skin.

My hands slid up and around his neck, and my fingers ran through the short hairs at the nape of his neck while the kiss sent spirals of ecstasy through me.

Slowly laying me down on the bed, Jacob removed the rest of my clothing before removing his own. As his flesh was revealed my eyes couldn't get enough of the stunning man. My man.

"Rose," he groaned as he watched me lick my lips while I stared at a part of him that was really very hard and looked painful.

"What you do to me," he muttered, chuckling with amusement.

Climbing onto the bed, he pulled me into his arms and started to trace his fingers lightly along my back, and moving down to my bottom, he squeezed, pulling me closer.

I held him against me and my whole body shuddered when I felt his excitement against my thigh.

Reclaiming my lips, he moved on top of me and nudging my legs apart, slipped between them. When he completely filled me, he wrapped me up in his arms so that there wasn't an inch between us.

I held his gaze and when he whispered, "I love you, Rose. You're mine, forever and always," I felt that my heart, well and truly, belonged to Jacob.

He slowly started to rock against me while he placed small kisses all over my face. The pleasure grew more and more intense between us as I gasped for breath and clung to his shoulders. He suckled one of my breasts into his mouth and that was all it took, and I shattered into a million pieces, seconds before I felt Jacob swell and twitch inside of me. Our love-making brought tears to my eyes.

He withdrew, keeping me in the circle of his arms while I settled against his chest.

Making love on the beach had been wonderful, but in Jacob's bed had been beyond that.

He moved slightly away but kept me in the circle of his arms while I settled against his chest.

"Rose?"

I lifted my head and searched his gaze because I sensed he had something important to ask me. "Yes?"

"If I manage to get an apprenticeship in Boston, will you really go with me? And be my wife?"

I burst into tears. "Yes, yes, yes." I kissed him all over his face in my excitement as my tears continued to flow.

Jacob helped me to mop up, laughing at my enthusiasm.

I laughed. "You only want to go to Boston because of the Boston Braves," I teased.

"That may be a factor." He winked.

Chapter 14

AFTER READING ABOUT THE LOVE BETWEEN ROSE AND Jacob last night, I wake feeling refreshed and light-hearted.

If only to have a love like they had—to know, once in a lifetime, what it would be like to love someone so much and for it to be returned.

Since Lucas has been spending time with Thomas, he's been falling asleep pretty soon after going to bed and waking up after me, much to her delight.

After my morning shower, I dress in my favorite shorts and head downstairs only to find Lucas already sitting at the kitchen table reading.

"I thought you were in bed," I comment, ruffling his hair as I walk past him to start the coffee.

"Thomas said he's going to come for breakfast again, so I didn't want to miss him."

I laugh. "Oh, Lucas. I can assure you that there is no way you would have missed him."

There's a knock on the back door, and seconds after, Lucas bolts out of his chair, running to answer it while I root around in the bottom of the refrigerator for some eggs.

"Auntie Mack, it's the very hot guy from next door," Lucas shouts, which has me banging my head on the refrigerator.

I quickly turn to see the gorgeous man from last night standing at my backdoor, his eyes doing some looking of their own.

"Oh!" is the first thing that comes to mind, and out of my mouth. I can't remember the last time I was so embarrassed. How am I going to get out of this one? *Pretend Lucas hadn't said anything.*

Which is what I do. "Hi, I'm Mackenzie Harper, but everyone calls me Mack."

He takes my outstretched hand, and I feel a spark of attraction race up my arm when our skin touches —the last thing I expected.

"Nice to meet you, Mack. I'm Dean Simone and I've moved in next door for a few weeks." His lips twitch with amusement, and I don't miss the look he passes over my body, his gaze hesitating over my legs.

Before anyone can respond, Lucas does, "She already knows. She was hanging out the window telling my mom on the phone when you arrived."

With a shocked intake of breath, I slap a hand over Lucas's mouth. "How many times have I told you not to listen to adult conversations?"

"It's a bit difficult when I'm in the room when you're having the adult conversation," Lucas replies with a huge grin, knowing exactly what he is up to.

At a loss for words, I hustle Lucas into the living room to play a game, hoping Thomas will arrive soon.

I turn around and catch Dean looking at my legs, again. He very slowly moves up my body, his eyes finally connecting with mine.

I'm flustered, thanks to him and Lucas. "Dean, what can I do for you? I presume you called around for a reason?" I ask in a husky voice.

The man appears lost in thought, as I question, "Dean?" embarrassed, as he gives me another once-over.

"Oh, sorry. I seem to have forgotten things like coffee, milk, and sugar. I was wondering whether you would take pity on your new neighbor and loan me some."

He has a killer smile, and I stutter in embarrassment. "That's fine. In fact, there's some fresh coffee over there if you want to help yourself to a cup."

"Great, thanks." He walks over toward the coffee, and while he pours a cup, his eyes track my every move.

I know he watches me as I start to cook breakfast.

Seconds later, Thomas walks through the backdoor with a bunch of tulips in his hands, making his way over to me, not noticing Dean as yet.

"Well, Mack, you look pretty good this morning. I think it's time you went and introduced yourself to the young man next door." He winks.

Dean clears his throat, trying not to laugh, causing Thomas to jump around in surprise. Dean smiles. "I'm Dean from next door," he introduces.

Thomas looks back and forth between myself and Dean. "I'm Thomas."

"Dean popped in to beg for coffee." I smile at Thomas and continue, "Breakfast won't be long. Lucas is waiting in the living room for you." I watch Thomas walk away, and then turn toward Dean. "Would you like to stay for breakfast?"

"Mmm, I'm hungry..." he comments, chuckling when my eyes pop open at the innuendo in his voice.

Blushing, I announce, "How about pancakes?"

"I love pancakes." He rubs his grumbling stomach.

I finish mixing the batter for the pancakes while I only half concentrate, as I find Dean's presence overwhelming in the small kitchen. He seems to permeate every single space.

"You can go relax in the living room and watch them play Lucas' game, if you'd like," I say, trying to get him out of the kitchen before I do something stupid.

"No, I'm fine right here...watching you."

Not knowing what to say, I turn my back to him and start cooking the pancakes.

Once made, I bend over to place the cooked pancakes into the oven to keep them warm, and closing the oven I turn, catching a strange look on Dean's face. Ignoring him, I move toward the table and place warmed syrup and butter in the middle before I call Lucas and Thomas into the kitchen for breakfast.

After I place the food and drinks on the table, the only seat left is the one next to Dean, so with a quick glance at him, I take the seat. Our eyes meet as he smiles over a forkful of pancakes, but it assures me that his mouth is at least busy.

Eating in silence, I feel flustered, and I keep telling myself it really has nothing whatsoever to do with the really hot guy sitting next to me. Unfortunately, his voice matches his body, and he is no doubt, used to using his voice to get women to drop their panties. Squirming in my seat from the hot glances Dean keeps throwing my way, I decide a distraction is needed before I jump the guy.

"Auntie Mack?" Lucas says, and for once his interruption is appreciated.

"Yes, Lucas?" I silently thank my nephew.

"Will you make me a cake today, please? If I promise to be good."

"I baked a pound cake yesterday. You can have a slice of that after dinner," I offer, feeling myself blush, and certainly not admitting I've made it for Dean. "Now eat up, so you can go off with Thomas."

I turn to Thomas, and ask, "What are you two up to today?"

He winks at Lucas. "Well, my buddy and I, thought we might dig for worms."

I have taken a sip of coffee, which ends up going down the wrong way as I start to choke. Putting the cup down rather heavily, it sloshes everywhere. I jump up to grab some paper towels, only to find Dean already on the case.

Actually, he's more interested in drying my legs than anything else.

"Dean, you about finished down there?" I stand with my hands on my hips, holding back amusement.

"I've not even started," he whispers.

I open and close my mouth, lost for words as Dean remains on his knees, flirting with me.

In the end, he takes pity on my blushing form, and quickly stands, taking his seat.

I glance across the table only to see both Thomas and Lucas watching the show. Thomas looks as though he's about to burst with laughter.

"Now where were we?" I ask once I'm seated again.

"Worms. They're to use as bait because Thomas dropped the others," Lucas announces with glee.

With a glare at both Thomas and Lucas, I can't decide if they are serious or not and from the look on Dean's face, neither can he.

"Where did you drop them?" I ask very slowly.

Both Lucas and Thomas look rather shifty. "I think it's time to go. Come on, Lucas."

"Okay, bye, Auntie Mack. Bye, Dean," Lucas shouts as he skips off in front of Thomas.

I lean forward and put my head in my hands then groan. "Those two!"

Dean laughs. "Are they always like that?"

"Pretty much."

I start moving the dishes from the table while Dean fills the sink with water and starts to wash them. I pick up a hand towel and dry them, still a bit stunned there is a sexy guy in my kitchen who doesn't disappear the minute he's finished eating—a keeper, as my mother would say.

It has been a really long time since anyone has flirted with me, and it feels really nice. The fact that Dean seems like a decent guy adds to the pleasure.

"Do you want to go for a ride on my bike?" Dean asks.

"You mean the Harley?" I ask with a huge grin on my face, pulling him out of his thoughts.

He winks. "Is there any other?"

"Give me five to put some jeans on."

As I race upstairs, I hear Dean groan before he clears his throat. I love his reaction to me.

Not five minutes later, I stand before him in jeans. "You ready?" I ask, already on my way out the door.

"Oh, yes," he whispers.

"What?"

With a small cough, he tries to clear the restriction in his throat. "Yes, let's go." He follows me outside, to where he's parked up.

Standing beside his bike, Dean lifts the spare helmet from the back. He fastens it securely under my chin as I move closer to the warmth of his large body, but once on the bike, I hesitate, having no idea where to place my hands.

"Hold the brackets here and here," Dean answers my unspoken question.

"Thanks."

"Or me." He grins before he puts his helmet on.

I take him at his word and slip my hands around his waist, my fingers edge beneath his T-shirt. I grin to myself as I feel his stomach muscles quiver—two can play the game.

Chapter 15

"THOMAS, WHAT DO YOU THINK AUNTIE MACK AND Dean are doing?"

He looked at Lucas, who was sitting in the lounge with cookies and milk, reading another *Our Gang* comic. "Um, talking. They are neighbors, you know," he replied.

"He seems okay. I think he likes Auntie Mack. Do you think he'll marry her and go live with her?"

He didn't really know where Lucas was going with that question. "Would that bother you if he did, Lucas?" he asked, taking a seat beside him.

Lucas stuck out his lower lip in a pout and said, "I wanted her to marry you."

He laughed. "Lucas, I'm an old man. Your aunt is

young and needs a younger man, like Dean or someone like him."

"Have you ever been married?" Lucas asked with a frown.

"Yes. I was married for thirty years before she passed away."

"That's sad." Lucas went quiet for a few moments. "What was her name?"

Thomas was deep in thought and replied, "Janet, the love of my life."

"Hmm, well, would you be my granddad then? Scott has three granddads, and he says it's really cool."

"We'll have to see, Lucas. Let's get back to reading. Do you want me to read you this one?" he asked, rather amused.

"Yes, please."

Be his granddad. If Lucas only knew how much he would really enjoy that. Hopefully, Mack would stay in touch with him when it was time for her to head back to Boston. He would miss them both terribly.

~

DEAN WAS AT THE PORTLAND HEAD LIGHT WATCHING Mack while she walked along the edge of the cliffs.

With the light breeze from the ocean blowing her hair back from her face, she was stunning.

He'd really enjoyed spending the day with her. They'd driven into Portland and browsed around the Old Port shops. Then on their way to the lighthouse, they'd stopped for lunch and ate a delicious lobster meal.

Dean, for the first time in a long time, felt as though he could breathe. Mack was like a breath of fresh air, so easy to talk to, to laugh with. She listened to what he had to say without interrupting, and only offered her opinion once he'd finished. And her opinions were rich and full of amazing insight. She even listened as he went on and on about his work as a graphic novelist. He worked with a couple of authors, who had great ideas, but couldn't put their vision on paper, which is where he came in. He loved his work and the flexibility it gave him.

They'd already walked around the lighthouse, and as they'd approached the cliff edge, he'd taken hold of her hand, lacing their fingers together.

Dean wanted that contact again as he walked over to where she waited for him. On his approach, she turned and when her gaze landed on him, she offered him a dazzling smile, causing him to miss a step. She was so beautiful with all that flowing brunette hair, and she took his breath away, especially when she smiled for him.

He stood in front of her without saying anything and moved his hands to her face in a light caress. He searched her eyes before he lowered his head and placed a light kiss to her lips. "You are so beautiful." He lowered his head again and used more pressure against her mouth. She moved in closer, wrapping her arms around his waist, allowing the kiss to deepen.

He shivered and groaned. "I think we better stop," he whispered, placing small kisses around her lips.

"Then why aren't we?"

He couldn't stop touching her, and smoothed his hands down her arms, moving them so his fingers could caress her waist under the T-shirt before he intertwined his fingers with hers. "Because I don't have any willpower with you. This top has been driving me crazy all day. Every time you move, I catch a glimpse of your stomach."

"I was so tempted to put my hands elsewhere when I sat behind you on your bike," she admitted, laughing, then she squeezed Dean's bottom before she took a step back.

"I don't know how I managed to get us anywhere without crashing while your hands were on me. Nothing has ever felt so good."

She winked at him. "I know." Then she sauntered toward his Harley. She knew damn well that his eyes were on her bottom the whole way.

"I hate to say this, but I think I better take you back."

Lightheaded with happiness, Mack laughed. "Mmm, Thomas will be waiting with Lucas."

"Their friendship is unique," Dean observed.

"Yes, it is."

I REMOVE MY HELMET, AND THEN HOLD MY ARMS OUT for Lucas who runs straight into them.

"Auntie Mack, have you really been on Dean's bike?"

"Yes, I have."

"That's not fair. I want to." Lucas starts to get tearful, although I know for a fact that Lucas is rather capable of putting on the waterworks at will.

"Hey, Lucas, you want to sit on the bike, and I'll

take you around the yard?" Dean asks him before the waterworks really start.

Lucas's tears instantly dry as he dives out of my arms and runs straight over to Dean, who lifts him astride the bike.

Dean winks at me before he turns his attention to Lucas. "You need your helmet on, young man." He laughs as Lucas stills with an eager grin on his face and allows Dean to place the helmet on his head.

I feel a bit unsure about Lucas being on the Harley, and walk closer to Dean, who catches the frown on my face. He takes hold of my hand and places a kiss to my cheek.

"He'll be fine, don't worry." He leans in to give me another quick kiss, on the lips this time before he climbs on the back of his bike. Dean surrounds Lucas with his body as he explains to him what the different instruments are for on the panel in front of them.

I walk over to the steps leading into the cottage and sits down beside Thomas. I blush slightly when I meet his gaze and see the knowing look in them.

"I see you made friends with the neighbor then?" He chuckles.

I grin. "Oh, yeah."

Dean switches the bike on and very slowly puts it

into gear and starts moving around the yard with an excited Lucas sitting in front of him. With a glance at me every time he passes, Dean winks, which really amuses Thomas.

"Thomas, do you like Dean?" I ask as Dean switches the bike off.

"I don't swing that way," He tries not to laugh at the stunned expression on my face, but fails miserably.

With a laugh, I nudge him with my elbow. "You know exactly what I mean."

"I only met him briefly this morning, but from what I can see and how he spoke to me, I would say he's one of the good guys."

"Thanks."

"Auntie Mack, Thomas, did you see me?" Lucas barely manages to get out before diving on me.

"We certainly did. You were pretty good."

"Thanks, Auntie Mack."

"He's great." Dean ruffles Lucas's hair. "Listen, I'm going to leave you guys for now. I have some things to take care of. I'll come around tomorrow if that's all right?"

I smile up at Dean, slightly disappointed that he

isn't staying for dinner. "We'll see you at breakfast, right?"

Grinning, Dean asks, "Was that an invitation?"

"Sure was."

"I'll be there," Dean replies, hesitating.

I turn to Thomas. "You going to eat dinner with us?"

"No, thank you. I'm meeting a couple of friends in town tonight, so I'll see you all at breakfast," Thomas says.

Dean takes hold of my hand and pulls me toward him. "Walk with me a minute?"

Thomas grins at the two of us and stands, taking hold of Lucas's hand. "Come on, Lucas. Show me that game you keep talking about before I leave." They enter the cottage to give Dean and Mack some privacy.

WALKING OVER TOWARD DEAN'S COTTAGE, HE DIDN'T know what to say, because all he really wanted to do was drag Mack inside and never let her go. He wondered where that thought had come from. It wasn't one he'd had before...ever...for anyone...and certainly not for a woman he'd only just met.

Pushing the thought aside, he turned to Mack, took her face in his hands, and brought her in close. She put her hands on his waist and moved in even closer.

His mouth covered hers hungrily and his tongue sent shivers of desire racing through them both. Mack reached up and curled her arms around his neck, pressing hard against his tall frame.

However, he pulled his mouth away, trying to catch his breath, which had gotten stuck at the back of his throat when Mack rubbed herself against him. He shuddered and groaned. "Mack, we have to... stop."

She dragged his head back down to meet her lips while he grabbed hold of her hips and brought her into closer contact with the throb behind his zipper.

It was Dean who broke the kiss, but only because he'd heard a throat being cleared.

"You're both giving me high blood pressure," Thomas shouted from the kitchen window.

They laughed, amused at the older man.

Dean placed her slowly back on her feet before he

stepped away. "I think you better go before I drag you inside."

With what appeared to be reluctance, he watched as Mack took a few steps, and then on unsteady legs started to walk to her own cottage. She looked back over her shoulder. "Promises, promises," she teased.

She entered her own cottage laughing.

Dean let out a frustrated sigh as he entered his. He hadn't lied to Mack when he said about dragging her inside. He'd only met her that morning and after spending most of the day with her, he knew she was special.

Her hair was soft and smelled of raspberries, her skin was lovely and smooth, and those freckles, he thought they were speckles of cinnamon sugar, and probably just as tasty.

However, at the back of his mind was the fact that he'd lied to her. He hadn't been honest about his name or about the reason why he was in Cape Elizabeth, and that bothered him. The desire that had sprung up between them had been unexpected to say the least, but before anything more serious could happen, he had to tell her the truth.

Chapter 16

April 5, 1947

Breakfast with my parents . . .

I SNUGGLED DOWN IN MY BED WHILE I THOUGHT ABOUT Jacob and how gentle he'd been last night. He had been so patient, so tender when he'd made love to me in his bed. He'd made me feel cherished and loved.

I'd promised to marry him and move to Boston. The thought echoed through me, and I couldn't stop the smile shining on my lips. I could hardly wait. I wanted to be with him desperately. My heart was filled with so much love and hope when I thought about my future with him.

When he'd walked me home last night, we'd talked about our plans for Boston. At first, we would rent one of the rooms that his sister had available in her boarding house. Apparently, she only rented rooms to married couples so to begin with, until we could marry, we would pretend. Jacob had already spoken to his sister about me, and she had agreed to let us stay together and treat me as his wife.

Smiling to myself in excitement, I finally dragged myself out of bed, rushed to the bathroom to avoid everyone in the house, and then back to my room to dress for work. I was actually dreading facing Mother and Father at breakfast. If I could avoid doing so, then I would.

I took a deep breath for courage before I walked out of my room and down the stairs.

"Good morning... Mother... Father," I said, acting as though nothing untold had happened last night.

I took my seat, where my breakfast was already waiting for me. While I buttered a piece of toast, my father cleared his throat. "Where did you disappear to last night?"

"Somewhere peaceful," I replied and started to eat.

"Rose, dear, we thought that it would be a good match between you and Richard. He would be able to look after you," Mother said, patting my arm, trying to justify what they'd done.

Father nodded. "Richard would be able to look after you very well. His family has more money than we'll ever see."

I pulled my arm out from under my mother's hand and scared at my father with a stubborn glare. "Father, I'm sorry, but I'm not going to marry Richard. As your only daughter, you should want me to marry for love and to someone who can make me happy by being with them. Money shouldn't be a factor at all."

"You need money to live, Rose," Father said, his words clipped, as his face grew red with irritation.

"That's why there are jobs. I intend to marry someone who doesn't mind getting his hands dirty, and who doesn't mind working for his money. I have no intention of marrying someone who spends all day frittering away the family inheritance and doesn't work a day in his life."

Pushing away from the table, I looked at both my parents. "Please don't expect me to marry him because I will always refuse." I stormed out of the room, collecting my jacket and purse along the way, and then began walking slowly to work.

Unfortunately, my slow walk to work didn't go as planned. No sooner had I left the front path, Richard pulled up beside me. "Rose, let me give you a lift to work."

I ignored him and carried on walking.

"Rose, please talk to me," he begged as he jumped out of the idling car and ran up to me. "I'm really sorry about last night. My father said something that made me do what I did."

I sighed. "Richard, I'm sorry, too. I think it would be for the best if we don't see each other again, for a while, that way your father won't get the wrong idea about us."

I walked past him, leaving him stunned behind me. Not long after, I heard his car screech away from the curb, obviously in a temper.

At the library, Mr. Young put me on the front desk, which could be even more boring than dusting shelves. Throughout the day, I helped around ten people.

It had just turned three when I looked up, having heard the door opening, and my heart missed a beat when I found Jacob's gaze on me.

Standing, I straightened my shoulders and cleared my throat. "Mary, can you watch the desk please? I need to visit the restroom."

Mary nodded.

I followed Jacob to the Philosophy section.

Jacob took hold of my face and pulled me to him for a soul-warming kiss. "I hated sleeping on my own last night after having you in my bed." He kept kissing all over my face and finally came back to my mouth, slipping his tongue between my lips.

"I can't wait for us to be in Boston...to wake up with you every day and to eat our meals together... Oh, Jacob, I'm so excited."

"My Rose."

He couldn't stop kissing me. Not that I complained.

"I better go. I'll see you again soon. Remember, I love you," he told me.

I stood and watched him walk away, and out through the door.

The rest of the afternoon went really slow. All I wanted was to be with Jacob.

Finally, after a very long day, I left work and walked slowly home. I followed the path by instinct with my thoughts completely on Jacob and what our life would soon be like in Boston.

I entered the house, and both my parents greeted me. I froze with dread and looked from one to the other.

"Rose, please come in here a minute, I have something to say," Father said.

Dreading what my father was going to say, I followed my parents into the front parlor.

"I've spent most of the day thinking about what you said this morning." He looked very ill at ease. "We really don't want you to be unhappy, and I'm sorry if we gave you the impression your happiness doesn't matter because it does. Richard seems to care for you, and he would be able to make sure you are well looked after. Even if he doesn't do anything." *Did my father smile?* "Saying all that, we do want you to marry well, so please don't get it in your head that just anyone will do because they won't."

I wasn't sure what they expected me to say to Father's little speech. "Thank you. May I leave?" Father looked ready to continue speaking but thought better of it and nodded his head stiffly.

April 7, 1947

My dreams are closer . . .

As I was checking a book out for Mr. Willis, I looked up and saw Jayne walking into the library. She made me laugh as she looked around to make sure Mr. Young wasn't lurking about anywhere. Something that she always did whenever she came into the library.

"Jayne, why aren't you at work?" I asked, leaning on the desk toward her.

"I'm on an errand for one of the bosses. What's going on with you? I have hardly seen you. You haven't been to any of the local dances like usual. Are you seeing that, what's his name, Jacob?"

I guess I didn't hide my shock very well, my face giving me away. JT always said I made a terrible liar.

"Are you out of your mind? What if your parents find out?" she exclaims.

My face fell. "I know what my parents are like, but I love him, Jayne. I don't want anyone else. I'm going to be with Jacob whether they agree or not. I intend on telling them soon, just not yet." I really hoped she wouldn't tell anyone.

Not long after Jayne had left, a student from the local school came in asking if I would help him with a paper on George Washington. I'd no sooner said goodbye to the grateful student when Jacob walked in. He came straight over to my desk.

"Are you free to meet me at my apartment tonight?" he whispered.

"Yes." His eyes caressed my face, and I fought the shudder that wanted to ripple through me.

"I'll see you later."

"Who was that?" Mary questioned, her eyes following Jacob's exit.

I didn't really want to tell her, she talked about everyone behind his or her backs and I didn't want her to talk about me. "He wanted to know if we had a new book he'd heard about." I turned my back to her and started collecting some books that needed to be returned to the shelves. Thankfully, Mary didn't ask me anything else.

I spent the rest of the day watching the clock, counting down the seconds to when I could be with Jacob. The day really dragged on, and once or twice, I nearly went to see Mr. Young to tell him I had woman problems. I didn't though and I stayed until closing.

After brushing my hair and applying more lipstick, I dashed out of the library and quickly walked to Jacob's apartment.

Jacob opened the door, took one look at me, and grabbed hold of my arm. He pulled me behind him and slamming the door in one smooth movement, he kissed me. He backed me into the wall, not an inch between us while he continued to kiss me until I became breathless. Holding him tightly around his neck, I felt his hands searching under my dress.

"I need you, Rose." His voice broke with huskiness.

"Yes."

He groaned.

He wasted no time and dragged my underwear down my legs and off. Seconds later, I heard the zipper on his pants go down before he reclaimed my lips. His hands grasped hold of my bottom, and as he lifted me up and onto him, I wrapped my legs around his waist, throwing my head back moaning. He felt amazing.

"This is going to be quick." Without pause, he started thrusting, and white-hot pleasure heated my blood.

Suddenly, I felt that burst of ecstasy—that rapturous delight. I couldn't stop convulsing and moaning while Jacob groaned and swelled inside of me before he shuddered.

He panted heavily into my neck while I caught my breath.

"I'm sorry. I shouldn't have taken you like that... up against the wall." He shook his head.

"Jacob, you can take me like that any time you want, as long as we're not in public... It was amazing," I said brazenly.

He laughed, helping me to get my feet back under me. Then he fastened his pants before he picked up my panties from the floor and held them out to me on a finger.

I WALKED OUT OF THE BATHROOM AND FOUND JACOB IN his living room. He took my hand. "I want to show you something."

After we were comfortable, he passed me a letter, "Read it," and sat beside me.

The letter was from an engineering company in

Boston, offering him an apprentice position that started on Monday, April 21st.

"Will you still come with me, Rose?" He looked so nervous.

"I love you, Jacob. I have already agreed to be your wife, so yes, I will still come with you. I'd go anywhere with you."

He sighed in relief.

"Do you think you could be ready to leave a week today on the 14th? It would be easier for you if we were settled in Boston before I start the job. Eleanor has said you can help her with a few minor things around the house during the day if you'd like."

I smiled at him. "I would love that, and I can hardly wait."

"The money is good so we can save up and find ourselves an apartment fairly quickly. Or if you want to stay longer at my sister's then we might be able to save for a deposit on our own home, but I would prefer that we get married fairly soon."

I pulled his head down to mine and kissed him ever so softly. "I would marry you tomorrow if it was possible."

We cuddled on the sofa, not talking for the longest of time, and then all too soon, I had to head home.

Jacob walked me part of the way while we made plans to meet at eleven, the night of the fourteenth—next Monday.

I planned to take some of my things to Jacob's apartment on Friday, and then whatever else I wanted, I would have to sneak them out with me on the fourteenth.

My biggest regret was that I couldn't take JT with me. I would miss him so much. *I love you brother.*

I will miss Mother and Father, but they have forced me to make this choice. If I thought for one minute they would accept Jacob, I would tell them about us.

Before going to bed, I needed to find a hiding place for my diary so no one would stumble across it and stop our plans.

I knew the perfect place.

I smiled to myself.

Chapter 17

I STRUGGLE TO GET ROSE AND JACOB OUT OF MY thoughts and thinking about them brings tears to my eyes.

"Hey, Mack," Dean says in greeting as he walks into the kitchen, heading straight for the coffee pot. He pulls up short when he sees my tear-stained face. Changing direction, he moves straight up to me, and after looking closely, wipes the tears away with his thumbs.

He removes the pan from the burner and turns it off as he pulls me into his arms. "Mack, what's wrong? Why are you so upset?"

I can't answer and just burrow my face deeper

into Dean's chest. I wrap my arms around his waist while I sob.

A few minutes later, I pull away and move to the sink to splash cold water on my face, stopping briefly as I hear Thomas outside talking, probably on his phone. "It's something and nothing. Please don't say anything?"

Dean nods and frowns. "Are you all right now?"

"Actually, I think I am, but a good morning kiss might make me feel so much better." I stand right in front of him with a soft smile on my lips while I search Dean's eyes. He doesn't disappoint and gently caresses my shoulders with his warm hands before he leans closer for a very quick kiss, too quick.

"Auntie Mack, are you really doing kissing things with Dean?"

"Oh!" I turn crimson while Dean grins and walks over to Lucas doing the high five thing.

"How's it going, champ?"

"Good. I slept in today," Lucas replies, trying to see out of the window, obviously looking for Thomas.

"Thomas will be in soon, Lucas. I think he's talking on his phone."

"I wish he'd hurry up."

No sooner has he spoken, the back door opens and in walks Thomas. "Morning, folks."

He walks over and hand me a bunch of peonies.

I lean over to give Thomas a big hug and a kiss on the cheek. "I think you need to marry me, Thomas." He's so sweet and will make an amazing grandfather.

"Hey, not funny. He can get his own girl. You're mine." Dean pulls me into his arms, laughing.

Suddenly, I'm all serious and look up at Dean. "Am I really?"

Dean stops laughing and caresses my face. He pushes the hair back from my forehead. "Mack, I've never felt like this before, but I'm starting to think, that maybe, yes, you are." He places a lingering kiss to my lips.

"Auntie Mack, are you making breakfast?"

Thomas chuckles. "I think she's distracted."

Flustered, I pull away from Dean and finish making breakfast while deep in thought.

I wonder what I'm doing. How did this happen? Why did this, with Dean, feel so right? Never in my life have I been so attracted to anyone. Dean has popped into my life twenty-four hours ago. How in the heck has he managed to get under my skin so quickly? When he kissed me, I practically swooned at his feet.

I finally compose myself and place the eggs, bacon, and biscuits onto the table.

"Can we eat without mentioning anything unpleasant?" I catch a slim smile hovering on Thomas's lips as I take my seat and start to load my plate with food.

"This looks great," Thomas compliments.

"Thank you."

Thomas looks rather tired. "How was your evening?" Perhaps that might explain it.

"Late night, but a good one. I won at poker, fifty bucks," he says rather proudly. "I don't think I've won that big since 1998."

I froze with my fork halfway to her mouth. "Are you serious?"

"Sure am. I think Lucas here is my good luck charm."

"My granny and gramps play strip poker. Is that what you played?"

Dean roars with laughter, which in turn has everyone else laughing, except for Lucas.

"What's so funny?" Lucas asks, baffled.

"Your granny and gramps playing strip poker, and no, that wasn't what I played," Thomas manages to reply.

"But why is that funny? Granny says—"

"Lucas, that's enough. Your breakfast is getting cold." Heaven knows what Lucas is about to say.

Lucas, not wanting to be hushed, carries on, "Auntie Mack, I was only going to say that Granny said she wasn't embarrassed about her body or the droopy parts at her age." He pauses to catch his breath. "What droopy parts does she mean, Auntie Mack?"

Both Dean and Thomas make a quick exit outside. I can hear Dean laughing on the other side of the kitchen door.

I giggle to myself and tell Lucas to ask his father.

I really needed to have a word with my mother, who is the most flamboyant person I have ever known. My mother still lived in the sixties and isn't bothered who knows it and she gets more outrageous year by year. Sometimes she forgets whom she's talking to as Lucas has just proved. No matter how much like our mother Melinda is, she would've hit the roof if she'd heard that comment.

I remember growing up with Melinda, how proper behavior was expected when we were in school. Our mother used to threaten to wash our mouths out with soap and water if we said anything impolite. Perhaps I needed to try that with our mother. Give her a taste of her own medicine.

With breakfast now finished, I move to the back-door to find Thomas and Dean sitting on the stoop. "Thanks for the help, guys."

Dean grins. "Is it safe?"

"It is and, for abandoning me, you get to wash the dishes." I motion to the dirty dishes.

Dean stands and kisses me.

"Lucas, what would you say if we go fishing this morning and then read some comics this afternoon?"

"Sounds cool."

Thomas held Lucas's hand as they walked over to his cottage to collect the rods from the front porch where he'd left them in preparation for the morning's adventure.

Thinking about Dean and Mack, he chuckled to

himself. He'd noticed them both glancing at each other all through breakfast. Things looked to be heating up there. They'd only just met yesterday, but they seemed so in tune with each other. Sometimes a man and woman could spend a lifetime together and never be truly 'together'. His mother and father came to mind. He really hoped everything worked out for Mack and Dean. They made such a promising couple.

"Thomas, do you know how to make a cake?" Lucas asked, breaking his train of thought.

He looked down to see him waiting for a response. "Why do you want to make a cake?"

"Auntie Mack."

Thomas raised his eyebrows. "Why? Is it her birthday?" She hadn't mentioned anything.

"No, but she always makes them for me so I thought I could make her one this time." He looked so hopeful as he added, "With your help."

"Hmm. Well, I think it would be safer if we buy one. It might be more like the blind leading the blind if we try to make a cake." Thomas grinned at Lucas, who looked ready to carry on discussing a cake, then obviously thought better of it.

"Okay, I guess."

They reached his cottage. "Let's try and catch

some fish for dinner instead." He collected the rods and his fishing basket, took hold of Lucas's hand again for the walk to the stream. It was his favorite fishing spot that he'd been coming to for more years than he cared to remember.

Chapter 18

I'M ALONE WITH DEAN, AND ALL I WANT IS TO FEEL HIS lips on mine or, even better, his hands on my body. Smiling to myself, I perch on top of the kitchen table, fluff my hair, stick my chest out, and smile in Dean's direction.

"Dean."

He turns and nearly drops the plate in his hands. "Mack," he croaks. "What—" He coughs, gulps, puts the plate to one side, and very slowly walks over to me. "You are causing havoc with my intentions, Mack. You know that?" Dean leans a breath away from my lips and places his hands on my hips.

I reach up to run my hands through his disheveled

hair, then smile when I feel a shudder work its way through him.

"Mack." He breathes heavily as his mouth covers mine hungrily. He forces my lips open with his exploring tongue, holding me in place while he devours the softness of my mouth.

I moan and tingle, wanting more as I wrap my legs around Dean's waist, pulling him against the ache between my legs.

"I'm not doing this," Dean pants, his lips still warm and moist from our kiss.

"Doing what?" I reply, innocently, while I burn with desire, an aching need, for another kiss.

Dean groans. "You know I want you, Mack, but I want to take things slow. I want to spend time with you."

"This is spending time with me," I interrupt with a pout.

Dean untangles himself and steps away, resting his back against the kitchen sink as he stares at me.

"You. Are. Lethal. I have no intention of going anywhere so we are going to spend time together… without sex getting in the way." Dean laughs at the look on my face. "For now, that is." I'm glad he added the latter, but I'm still not happy to stop.

"You're serious, aren't you?"

"Yep." He crosses his arms over his chest and waits me out.

"Oh, all right then. What do you want to do?" His eyes flare at her question, which I catch and snicker. "Just remember exactly whose idea it was to put a stop to the hanky-panky."

"I won't forget. Let's grab our jackets and climb on the Harley."

AFTER WE SPENT THE MORNING DRIVING ALONG coastal roads, we arrived home to sounds of laughter coming from the direction of the beach. Dean takes my hand and leads me down the short path to the beach.

I smile, sliding my hand out from Dean's, I move in closer, wrapping my arm around his waist as Dean drapes his arm around my shoulders.

"You feel good against me, Mack."

"I know," I smirk.

"Dean!" Lucas shouts before the Frisbee clonks Dean on the head.

I burst out laughing as Dean takes off running

after a laughing Lucas, who ends up falling over because he's giggling so much.

"Stop. Stop. Stop."

"Are you sorry?" Dean asks him while they both wrestle in the sand.

"It wasn't me."

Dean freezes. "Are you telling me that you didn't throw the Frisbee at my head?"

Lucas nods and points toward Thomas.

Dean glances at Mack who is openly laughing. He stands, brushing the sand off his jeans, and then starts walking toward Thomas with Lucas running behind him screaming for Thomas to run.

Before Dean can get to Thomas, Lucas tackles him from behind, which sends them both sprawling in the sand.

Dean can't hold his laughter in anymore and grabbing Lucas, gives him a quick tickle, and then gets them both upright.

"Lucas, I wasn't about to tackle Thomas to the sand."

Lucas looks from Dean to Thomas. "You weren't?"

"No, but I did think we could have some fun and maybe get Thomas to sit over there, while you bury his feet in the sand for letting me think it was you with the Frisbee."

"Hmm, I think I like that idea. I need some ants."

I hold my laughter but when I look at Thomas I can't anymore and I join Dean and Lucas with my own chuckle. "The sand will be enough...this time," Dean tells Lucas with a wink.

"Oh, all right."

Dean pulls me into his arms as we watches Lucas take hold of Thomas's hand. It's so sweet watching the little boy take the older man to the place Dean had suggested. Thomas laughs as he sits down and watches Lucas bury his feet.

"They're really going to miss each other when we go back to Boston."

"We're not too far away in Boston. It's only a couple of hours, we can bring him back to visit," Dean replies, grinning when I realize he'd said 'we'.

I kiss him quickly on his lips and snuggle into his chest. "I like the sound of that."

"Thought you might," he mumbles sitting on a large rock with me in his arms. "I love watching them two together."

I chuckle. "They're a right pair and I'm sure that

Thomas still has the mischievous little boy still inside of him."

"Some of us never grow up Mack," Dean whispers, "and I think I'll let you discover whether or not I did."

Mack turns in his arms and after placing a tender kiss to his cheek, rests her head against his chest, and admits, "I don't care either way, Dean."

Chapter 19

THE PAST WEEK HAS FLOWN BY WITH ME AND DEAN spending most of our time together. Occasionally, Thomas and Lucas would tag along with us in my car. Lucas preferred to spend his time with Thomas, who sometimes would take him to meet up with Walt and Levi. That had left me and Dean alone more often than not so we spent our time cuddled together on the beach or, in the evenings, on the sofa. We had taken the time to get to know each other more. Dean had spoken about his love of drawing and art while I had spoken about the joys of being a teacher to a mischievous class of seven-year-olds.

I will really miss Thomas when the summer is over, and leaving Thomas, will probably break

Lucas's heart. At least with Lucas constantly being entertained he hasn't missed his parents as much as I'd thought he would. In fact, he's hardly spent time with me since we arrived. I'm not too bothered because of the wonderful friendship he's found with Thomas. Lucas talks to his parents' on the phone most nights, and he goes over his antics of the day with them.

Today, he's gone fishing again with Thomas, and they've planned to read some more comics while I haven't even picked up Rose's diary in a week. I've been too exhausted and giddy after spending my days with Dean.

"Spend the day with me?" Dean asks, making me jump, as I was lost in thought.

He walks over to me as I glance. "I'd like that. Do you want to go to the beach? I thought we could take a picnic with us. I want to tell you about something."

"That would be great."

As I pull a small picnic together, Dean walks over and takes a blanket from the drawer. Tucking it under his arm, he picks up the picnic basket and holding my hand we head down to the beach.

During the walk, I wonder whether I'm making the right decision, trusting a guy I've only known for a short period of time. He's certainly the first guy to get my libido to sit up and take notice from the get-go. That has never happened to her before so perhaps it's an omen.

I lead Dean over to the sheltered section of beach, which I've come to favor over the past few weeks, wondering if it's the same part of the beach that Rose and Jacob claimed so many years before.

Dean unfolds the blanket as I set the beach mats with the back supports built in on top of them—these are the best purchase I've made in a long time. I loved sitting on the beach and reading. With this support, I'm rather comfortable and can sit for hours.

Dean sits down and reclining against one of the mats, he holds his hand out for me. I reach into my purse for the diary, and then snuggle into a comfortable position between his legs, resting against his chest. He wraps his arms around me while we enjoy the peace and quiet for a few minutes.

I break the silence. "The day after we moved into Rose Cottage, I was placing some boxes on top of the cabinets in the kitchen and found this." I show him the diary. "When I opened it, the first page says, *'This is the diary of a Rose, March 4, 1947.'*"

"Wow, that's some time ago."

"I know. I've been reading it, and it's a love story between Rose and a young man by the name of Jacob Evans."

I feel Dean still and I give him a quizzical look. "Carry on, it's interesting," he says.

"It's so sad, Dean. They didn't even know each other more than two months when she died trying to run away with him to Boston."

Silence goes on longer than I expect, so I question, "Dean?"

"Yeah." He leans down and places a kiss on my forehead.

"The part that upsets me the most is that the night Rose died, Jacob had no idea she'd passed away. All these years, her family led him to believe she married someone else."

"Seriously?" he exclaims.

"She was on her way to meet him when she died. A few days later, Jacob called to ask about Rose and her father told Jacob that she had stayed and married this other man, Richard. He told Jacob that she didn't want anything to do with him. So, all these years, he's believed she chose someone else."

"That's so sad, Mack."

"Exactly. I found him. Jacob Evans. He's ninety

and lives in Brookline, Boston. I left a message with his housekeeper, but he hasn't gotten back to me yet. I know he's married, but I need to tell him that Rose really did love him. I need to tell him that she died before meeting him that night."

I turn my face toward Dean. "Thomas is Rose's brother. She referred to him in her diary as JT. He told me what his father said to Jacob on the phone. Do you think that I'm right in wanting to tell Jacob about Rose? It really does break my heart."

He stares into my eyes, which swim with tears. "Come here." He pulls me closer and uses his thumbs to wipe my tears away.

"Yes, I do." He inhales deeply. "I'll help you see Jacob Evans because I'm—"

"Auntie Mack, look at the size of this fish," Lucas shouts, running toward us on the beach.

I stand and start heading toward Lucas, and say over my shoulder, "Thanks, for listening."

I run over to Lucas. "That is huge." Then I stop short. "Is it dead?"

"Don't be silly. Of course, it's dead." Lucas replies in disgust.

I laugh at the indignation on his face. "Would you both like a sandwich?"

I drop down on the blanket as Dean starts to wrestle on the sand with Lucas. I wish this was my family. That's something I've never wished for before, with anyone else, until now. Reading Rose's diary has made me long for that kind of love and commitment.

There is something real happening between me and Dean, although we don't know a great deal, if anything, about each other. Over the past week, I've mentioned family, but for some reason he always changes the subject. Although, on one or two occasions, Lucas had interrupted.

"No thanks, Mack. We'll leave you two alone. We're going to put the fish in the fridge, have lunch, then more comic reading." Taking hold of Lucas, Thomas pulls him along.

"Bye, Auntie Mack. Bye, Dean." Lucas waves.

"See you later, champ." Dean smiles at Lucas as he ruffles his hair.

"We'll see you both later then," I say.

With an odd look on Dean's face, he asks, "Tell me about yourself, Mackenzie?" He takes hold of my hand and tugs me down to cuddle into his side with my head resting on his shoulder and his arm around me.

I smile, inhaling deeply. "You already know some of this but let me refresh your memory. Mackenzie Louise Harper is twenty-seven years old and a teacher from Roslindale, Boston. Her parents are Louise and Alex Harper, who are fifty-nine and sixty-five years old, respectively. They live in a retirement village on the North Shore after spending more than thirty-five years teaching high school. My sister, Melinda, is four years older than me and married to a doctor, Daniel. They only have the one son, Lucas. I'm not divorced, married, and I'm in a relationship with you. I think that about covers it. What about you?"

He inhales. "Mack, my name is Dean James... Evans."

I still in his arms at hearing *Evans* from his lips.

He continues, "My mother's maiden name is Simone. I'm a graphic novelist, and my sister, Alice, is five years older than me and married to Simon, who's in financing."

He takes a trembling breath. "I'm thirty-two, never been married. My parents are Anne and James, who are sixty-five and sixty-eight years old, respectively. They live with my grandparents in Brookline... They are Jacob and Eliza Evans."

"Oh," I whisper, so quietly I'm not sure he heard me.

"Mack, did you hear me?"

"Yes," I murmur.

"I wanted to tell you the minute the name Simone left my mouth, and I don't know why I didn't, or rather I didn't want to look like an idiot in front of a woman I couldn't take my eyes off. I'm truly sorry, Mack."

"Why?" I hug my knees and gaze out at sea.

"My grandfather made a lot of money, and so did my father, for that matter. People get ideas about it and contact us for various reasons, sometimes shady reasons. When I heard Martha on the phone with you, I told her that I would check you out first. I knew the minute I saw you that you weren't in that category, but I'm so worked up over you and want you like crazy that I can't kiss you again until you know the truth."

He pauses and then continues, "After listening to you earlier, I think my grandfather really is your Jacob Evans. I have an Aunt Rosalind. Could he have named her after Rose?"

"Seriously?" I ask.

"Yes."

After what feels like an hour of silence but is only five minutes, I take hold of Dean's hand and lace my fingers with his. "Thank you for telling me. I'm glad you told me now, rather than later," I admit, blushing.

Dean moves in close. "Am I forgiven?"

"Is that the only untruth you've told me?"

He looks slightly sheepish. "I really am in this relationship with you." He declares. "But my mother is trying to marry me off to her friend's daughter, Cynthia. That's one of the reasons why I decided to check you out. I needed to get away from her matchmaking. I was glad I did the moment I met you."

"Cynthia?"

He sighs. "Yeah. My mother decided she wanted grandchildren, and my sister refused to cooperate, so she focused on me. Cynthia's mother has been friends with mine since school, and as we're of a similar age and background, they decided to push us together."

He glances at me. "I'm not interested in Cynthia. In fact, she's starting to annoy me, always showing up wherever I am. No one but Martha knows I'm here right now, and I plan to keep it that way. You're the only one I want, Mack."

I smile and brush the hair from his forehead.

"Thank you for telling me. What was the other reason?"

He offers an embarrassed smirk. "Curiosity, after your message. I love my grandparents, so I'll take you to see him and distract my grandmother while you speak with him."

I frown and he continues, "They go everywhere together, always have and always will, I guess," he swallows back the lump in his throat, "when one passes away, the other one will follow not long after, I'm certain."

I gently use my fingers to wipe the tears away from her eyes. "Oh, Dean."

I climb astride him and take hold of his face, then place a light kiss to his lips. "That is so sweet and heartbreaking at the same time."

"Yes, it is." He moves close, his tongue tracing along the soft fullness of my lips. I give myself freely to the passion of his kiss and hearing him groan is a heady sensation.

Desperate for more of him, I wriggle further onto his lap, where I come into contact with his pulsing length. I run my hands through his hair, deepen the kiss even further, and rub myself on him.

Dean pulls away, breathless. "Hell, Mack. We have

to stop because I'm seconds away from taking you here on the beach."

I place a light kiss against his lips. "I want that, too." Dean's eyes flare. "Lucas could reappear. Heck, what am I thinking? We're on an open beach, you made me forget," I shyly confess.

He rests his forehead against mine. "I know."

I climb off him and avoid looking into his lap. "Do you want me to read some of the diary to you?"

"That would be great." He pulls me in beside him.

"I must warn you, there's some racy writing in it." I laugh at the look on Dean's face.

"Can't we miss those bits?"

"No, we cannot," I grin slyly. "Those are the best bits."

Chapter 20

April 9, 1947

Jayne went out with Richard . . .

TODAY WAS A LOVELY, SUNNY DAY, AND FOR THE FIRST time in a long time, I was actually looking forward to going to work, or I was, until Jayne called around to the house to walk to work with me.

She took a long look at me, and asked, "Why are you so grumpy this morning?"

"Work," I replied. I thought it was better keeping to myself how much I was looking forward to walking to work on my own so I could get lost in my thoughts.

"I went out with Richard last night," Jayne said so quickly that I almost didn't catch what she'd said.

I raised my eyebrow when she stopped talking, waiting for her to tell me how it went. It wasn't like Jayne to keep anything to herself, especially about her dates.

She sighed. "All he did was talk about you. He's really angry that you refused his marriage proposal, and I think he only asked me out to try to make you jealous. When I told him it wouldn't work, he declared it was time to take me home."

I hadn't been expecting that. I actually thought he only wanted to marry me because of his father, but perhaps that was what he wanted me to believe. I rubbed my temples, feeling really confused. "Jayne, I'm not interested in Richard. In fact, the last time I saw him, I told him I didn't want to see him for a while. I was so angry with him for talking to Mother and Father."

"Are you still seeing Jacob?" My silence spoke a thousand words. "Rose Degan, you have to stop right now. Your father will make your life miserable if he ever finds out."

"I can't stop seeing him. I'm in love with him," I admitted, close to tears.

"Richard asked me last night if you were seeing someone else. I avoided the question, but it won't be long until he finds out." She saw the look on my face. "It won't be from me, I promise you," Jayne assured me.

She hugged me briefly before we parted outside of the library. She worked one block over from me and I watched her stroll down the street...another person I would miss when I left. I really hoped Richard didn't cause any trouble. I only had five days left in Cape Elizabeth, and I really wanted them to go smoothly.

My parents had been leaving me alone, and I really hoped they continued to do so.

April 10, 1947

A strange day ...

THIS MORNING UPON WAKING, I HAD TO RUN TO THE bathroom to be sick. *Yuck.* I ate dry toast and sipped on some water, which seemed to help some. With my stomach settled, I had a slow walk to work.

As soon as the library doors were unlocked, Richard had stalked in. He'd given me a glare before going to find whatever book he'd come in for. Soon after I noticed him about to leave, he'd stopped by the exit, his head turned toward me. He stared in anger, muttering to himself before he stormed out.

His behavior was odd. After what Jayne had told me yesterday, I still found it hard to believe. He'd seemed so genuine when he'd said it was his father making him ask me to marry him. Now I really didn't know what to think.

"Rose, can you come into my office for a moment, please?" Mr. Young asked, taking my mind off Richard.

"Of course." I followed him into the small box room that he called an office.

After he'd cleared his throat a few times—*horrid*—he looked at me. "Take a seat." I sat down stiffly. "Rose, I'm afraid I have to cut your hours. The library isn't as busy so I can't justify having as many staff." He sat staring at me.

I wasn't sure what he wanted me to say. "From when are the new hours starting?" I inquired politely.

He seemed relieved. "From May 6th."

I would be gone by then.

Only four more days to go. I felt so apprehensive, but excited, for my new life with Jacob.

Before going to bed, I'd played cards with JT, who was so infuriating. He cheated—*all the time*.

I really wished I could take my brother with me. I would miss him more than anyone.

April 11, 1947

A delightful discovery . . .

I WAS SICK AGAIN THIS MORNING. COULD I POSSIBLY BE pregnant? I didn't have any experience with this kind of thing and couldn't exactly ask my mother. *Heaven forbid.* I had some toast for breakfast again, which seemed to help calm my stomach.

I was meeting Jacob this evening with some of my things. I loved him so much and couldn't wait to see him. Before I left for work, I packed as much as I could into my travel bag, then stuffed it into the back of my wardrobe and prayed it wouldn't be discovered while I was at work.

How I got through the day, I would never know. Mr. Young had a bee in his bonnet and did nothing but fuss the whole day. I actually felt like a wilted flower as I walked home. He had us running around, doing this, that, and the other. Nothing was right, and as soon it was time to close, Mary, Emma, and I, had stopped what we were doing, retrieved our jackets and purses, and left in haste.

Dinner with my parents was a silent affair. JT had been in trouble again. I'm not sure what he'd done this time, but no one spoke. It was pretty horrible really. Excusing myself, I dashed up to my room and retrieved my travel bag.

Luckily, my bedroom overlooked the back garden and Mother's rose bushes, so I stuck my head out of the window to check that the coast was clear and dropped my bag. I prayed it didn't land in the middle of the roses.

I slipped out of the house, having snuck down the kitchen stairs, and retrieved my bag. The roses were intact. Thank goodness.

I walked to the end of the drive and found Jacob there waiting for me. I dropped my bag to the ground and threw myself into his arms. "I've missed you," I whispered.

His lips met mine. The kiss lingered. He tasted divine.

We breathed heavily when we finally parted, and Jacob took my hand while we walked into town. I should have been bothered about my parents seeing us, but I wasn't. In town, Jacob pulled me into a photography studio.

"What are we doing in here?" I asked.

He smiled at me. "I want a photograph of us both. We'll get two copies so you can give one to your brother."

I had tears in my eyes as I followed the photographer through to the back of the shop. Jacob stood behind me with his hands wrapped around my waist. I cuddled into him as the photographer snapped our moment in time. The man used a Polaroid Land Camera, which he said he was testing for a friend before they became available to the public. It produced our photographs in minutes, like magic.

With two photographs safely in his pocket, we continued on to his apartment. Jacob placed my bag down by the side of the chair in the living room.

He turned, cupping my face between his warm

palms. Firstly, he kissed the tip of my nose, then my eyes, and, finally, he kissed my waiting mouth.

"Make love with me." I didn't hesitate as I took him by the hand and led him into his bedroom.

He undressed me in slow, sweeping caresses and laid me on his bed, his eyes burned with desire. He started to remove his clothes, which I found delightful as I watched his muscular frame appear— he had an amazing body.

He laid down next to me as I rolled to my side. "I want to touch you," I whispered softly.

He gulped. "I hope I survive." He watched me through heavily lidded eyes as I sat up and smoothed my hands over his chest. I felt his eyes on me as I followed a path down to his ribs and then back up to the tight buds of his nipples. Leaning over him, I swirled my tongue around one of the hard nubs and felt him shudder.

Slowly, I caressed over his ribs, following with my lips, and when I reached his erection, I gently stroked along the hard length, enjoying the unfamiliar texture, before I wrapped my hand around him, feeling him pulse against my palm. A garbled moan hissed between his lips when I rubbed my thumb around the crown, where he leaked, and I watched as he arched off the bed in obvious pleasure. I felt daring and brave having watched his reaction to my touch, so I dipped my head and licked the bead of moisture that pooled on the flared head before I licked along the full length of him.

He panted, clutching at the sheets under him. "Enough...you have got to stop," he mumbled, rising over me. He caressed my face with his hands while my core quivered at the feel of him sliding inside of me.

He slammed his lips down onto mine, slipping his tongue into my mouth while he started moving his hips in a slow, seductive rhythm. He started to nibble my neck, moving further south. He took one breast into his mouth then moved to the other one. His thrusts sped up and seeing stars, I lunged against Jacob, who started to groan as he jerked inside of me.

Breathing heavily, still joined, he wrapped his arm around my waist and rolled onto his side.

"I love you so much, Rose," he whispered.

"I love you as much... I have something to tell you, and I hope you'll be as happy as I am."

Jacob searched my gaze and must have seen the hesitation in my eyes. "You can tell me anything, Rose."

I held his gaze and confessed, "I think I'm pregnant."

He froze beside me, and then turned away.

I could feel my eyes filling with tears as I watched him shut me out.

"Jacob?"

He sighed and dropped his head into his hands.

I couldn't stay. I needed to leave. I started to move toward the door, when Jacob caught hold of my wrist, pulling me into his arms.

"I'm sorry, Rose. I wasn't expecting you to say that. It was a shock." He gradually started to smile, which spread across his face. "Rose, not only have you given me your love, but you've given me the most amazing gift...a child. I promise, I will always love you, and provide for you and our child...children."

He stroked my stomach tenderly. I watched him with silent tears cascading down my face while happiness overwhelmed me at what I'd found with Jacob, my Jacob.

"Let's leave tonight," he said so seriously.

"We can't. I'm not ready tonight, but I will be on Monday."

He pulled me tight against his chest. "I want you with me."

"I want that as well. It's only three more days." I kissed him.

He made love to me, then we dressed, and he walked me home. I hated parting from him. I wanted to stay wrapped in his arms.

April 12, 1947

Richard was sneaking around . . .

I WAS SO SICK THAT I COULD BARELY MOVE. THERE could be no mistake. I was pregnant. I found myself unable to wipe the smile from my face. I was so happy, and my new life with Jacob was only two days away.

At work, I found myself humming while I placed returned books back onto the shelves. I got some strange looks from my colleagues, but I didn't really care.

Richard walked into the library and stared at me. Other than the other day, I had no recollection of him coming in before. He actually made me feel uncomfortable. If I didn't know better, I'd say he was up to something. I prayed it didn't involve me, but I couldn't think of any other reason for his behavior. I had a really bad feeling.

Dinner tonight was, yet again, a rather quiet affair as JT had been grounded again. He had been caught pinching an apple pie from Mrs. Jenkins next door. Apparently, she had left the pie by the window to cool, and JT and his friend, Levi, had taken it, hoping she would think it was a dog, but she had caught them taking the plate back.

April 13, 1947
Only one more day . . .

I FELT A BIT BETTER THIS MORNING, AND MY BREAKFAST stayed down, thank goodness. I walked out of the front door and bumped into JT, who was sulking because he wasn't allowed out after yesterday's fiasco with the pie. Father had told him, school, and home with nothing in between. I could guarantee that by the time he arrived home this afternoon, he'd be in more trouble.

At the library, Richard came back and actually walked over to me. "Rose, I want to speak with you."

Well, nice to see you too.

He took hold of my elbow and pulled me along roughly out of hearing range of anyone who might have come along. "What does he have that I don't?"

"What?" I asked, stunned. Surely, he couldn't be referring to Jacob. Could he?

"I saw you two days ago. You were wrapped around a tall guy. You were acting like a...like a... hussy."

The nerve of him. "What I was doing and, with whom, is none of your business," I told him, walking away.

He grabbed my arms and turned me around. "If you continue to see him, I'll tell your parents. I bet they don't know, do they?"

"You have no right interfering in my life. Who I have a relationship with is my business, not yours or my parents. So please stay out of it."

He turned away from me and headed toward the exit. Tossing a sneer over his shoulder, he said, "We'll see, Rose. We'll see."

For the first time since I'd met Jacob, I felt really scared and was afraid all of our happiness was about to come tumbling down. I really wished Jacob was with me, to hold me and tell me everything would be all right.

After lunch, I got my wish. I heard the front door open and glanced up, meeting Jacob's eyes. He took one look at me and obviously knew there was something wrong. I stood and followed him to the back of the library, near the storage closet. I walked past him, took his hand, and pulled him after me into the closet.

"What's wrong? Are you sick?" he asked me with concern all over his face.

I shook my head and burrowed my face into his chest. "Richard came in this morning. He said if I didn't stop seeing you, he would tell my parents." I looked up into his face. "He saw us kissing the other night."

"Nobody threatens you, Rose. Do you hear me? I'm going to go see him."

Oh, no!

"Jacob, please don't. Knowing Richard, he'll report you to the police, and then you'll get arrested, and we won't be able to leave tomorrow."

While I held him tight, I stayed silent. I wanted him to cool his anger and calm down.

As he pulled away from me, he stroked my stomach then knelt down. He wrapped his arms around my hips and kissed my stomach, which brought tears to my eyes. I didn't know what I'd done to deserve him, but I was so grateful.

He stood and kissed my lips. "I better go before I get you into trouble."

I grinned.

"Um...any more trouble." He chuckled, amusement clear in his gaze. "Everything is set for tomorrow night so don't worry."

"I won't. I'm really excited too finally be with you."

We snuck out from the cupboard, and I picked a couple of books up from one of the shelves to make it look as though I was returning them. I watched Jacob leave, and then rounded the corner to the next aisle where I bumped into Mary.

"That's the same man as before. Are you sure you don't know him?"

Mind your own business. "No, I don't know him."

Work was over for the day, for which I was grateful. After Jacob's visit, Mary kept watching me. She knew I was lying to her, and her constant gaze was very unnerving.

I took my time walking home because I knew that if I rushed, I would be in time to see Mother and Father before they went out. Luckily, I'd managed to miss them. I really hoped Richard hadn't been to see them. I was leaving tomorrow evening, but I wouldn't put it past him to cause a great deal of trouble for Jacob and me.

I entered the house through the kitchen and froze. JT was in the kitchen, stuffing his face with cookies and ice cream. "Have you eaten dinner?"

"Yes." He carried on eating.

"You're going to be sick."

He gave me a chocolate-covered grin. "I have an iron stomach."

"Ha, you wish." I made myself a sandwich and sat down with him.

Once finished, I helped him eat the cookies, dipping them into a glass of milk.

I really wished JT were a bit older so I could confide in him.

Chapter 21

I STOP READING AND CLOSE THE DIARY. I'M NOT SURE IF I will be able to continue. There is only the last entry left to read, the one that changes everything.

"Mack, what's wrong?" Dean asks as he sits and massages my shoulders.

I reach back to cover his hands with mine and lean into his chest. "I'm nervous to continue, knowing it ends with Rose's death." I wipe at a wayward tear with my fingers.

Dean wraps his arm around my waist and rests his chin on my shoulder. "Don't you want to know what happened on her last day?"

"Yeah," I whisper.

"Do you want me to read it?" Dean offers.

I let out a sigh. "No. I'll be okay. Let's eat and then we'll read about the fourteenth."

"Okay." Dean reaches for the picnic hamper. "Cheese or ham?"

"Ham, please."

I take the sandwich from Dean and sit resting my chin on my drawn-up knees, looking further along the beach while I ate. There is another couple who are playing Frisbee with two children as a dog runs circles around them. I hear the children giggling from where I sit.

"They look happy," Dean comments, following my gaze.

"I want that one day. To be part of a family unit that vacations at the beach." Holding Dean's gaze, I continue, "Don't you? Or do you enjoy being a single guy?" Even as I ask the question I know that I'm getting far more personal than a lot of people would prefer, but I'm really interested in how he sees his future.

Instead of ignoring me, Dean caresses down the side of my face before tracing his fingers over my lips. "Until I met you, Mack, I never even thought that far ahead, now that's all I'm doing." He smiles. "Yes, I see that family down the beach as being us one day, except," he smirks, "I kind of see maybe four or five kids running around with two dogs."

My eyes widen before amusement lights my face. "Four or five kids, huh?"

"Well, I guess six would be okay too." He laughs as I poke him in the chest. "You like that idea as much as I do," he suggests and catches my prodding finger. He brings my hand up to his lips and kisses my palm before closing my fingers over the kiss. "One day, Mack."

I search his eyes and happy with what I see, I turn back to look at the ocean as I finish the sandwich, and then dusting the crumbs from my lap, I turn and kneel between Dean's legs.

I wiggle my brows as I move closer. Dean's eyes widen when I reach for the bottom of his T-shirt. "I need distracting for a few minutes, and I want to have a closer look at the tattoo I keep catching glimpses of."

He grins. "Mack." I climb onto his lap and manage to pull the T-shirt over his head. Dean doesn't protest too much.

"Mmm, nice." It's my turn to grin.

I kiss him on the lips before I crawl out of his lap and around to the back of him.

On his back, from one shoulder to the other, spreads an eagle. It's magnificent, like nothing I've ever seen before. I reach out and start to trace the wings with my fingers. Dean breaks out in goose-bumps as I move closer and start kissing my way across the wingspan.

"Mack," Dean hisses. "We have a diary to finish," he whispers, his voice tight with tension.

I smirk, knowing exactly what I'm doing to him, but I give him peace by crawling back around to the front of him, unable to miss the bulge in his lap. "Your eagle is amazing."

He smiles. "I drew up the design and the tattoo artist did an excellent job of transferring it onto my skin."

"That he did. The design is amazing. You're really talented, but you knew that already."

"Hearing it out of your mouth makes it all the more real."

"You have an amazing talent, one that I've always been envious of...tell me about one of your projects. You're favorite one."

"That's an easy one." He grins. "It's one that I did for a paranormal graphic novel. My artwork is some of the best that I've ever done in that book. It was gothic, but detailed. I gained a lot more work after that book, which is still doing well in sales. I'll have to treat you to a copy as soon as I can."

"I'd love that." I become wistful. "Let's finish the diary."

I quickly kiss him and scoot back between his legs.

"Thank you for taking my mind off Rose and Jacob for a short while."

"If you carry on wiggling that bottom where you're wiggling it, you're going to get more of a distraction than I think you'd planned for."

"That really is a tempting offer. I've always wanted to make out on the beach. We'll have to take a rain check for when it's dark." I turn my head, laughing when I look into Dean's lust-filled expression. "Fun's over...for now." I reach for the diary.

Chapter 22

April 14, 1947

Today's the day . . .

ON MY WAY DOWNSTAIRS, I FELT REALLY WELL OR, AT least I did, until Mother asked me to join them for breakfast.

I entered the dining room and could tell straightaway that something was wrong. JT wasn't there, which meant he'd been told to eat in the kitchen.

"Who is this man you've been seen with?" *Heck.* So, Richard had been to see them.

I decided to be as honest as I could. "I have fallen

in love with a good man, and he's asked me to marry him." I paused and looked up at them. "I've agreed. I love him with all my heart."

Father looked ready to burst. "If he's a good man, why hasn't he been to ask me for your hand in marriage?" he roared.

"Because I asked him not to," I said quietly. Father was such a snob.

"Why?" he sneered.

I took a deep breath. "Because Jacob doesn't have a lot of money. He has an apprenticeship awaiting him in New York. I love him and want to be with him. I was afraid you wouldn't understand, and that you would prevent me from seeing him." The apprenticeship was in Boston, but that would be my secret for now.

"So, you keep saying you love him, yet you're ashamed to bring him to meet your parents?" Father threw his napkin down on the table.

"I'm not ashamed. Frightened, yes, but never ashamed!" I exclaimed.

I was as stubborn as my father when I wanted to be, but I stopped short of admitting that I was ashamed of my parents and how snobby they were.

"Then prove that to me, bring him to dinner tonight." Both Mother and I sat in shock.

"If you're serious, then I will."

"I'm serious. Seven this evening, we'll meet this young man you say you love." Father sneered.

I turned and stomped out of the house. I was halfway to work before I realized I hadn't eaten breakfast. I felt slightly dizzy, so I stopped at Belle's to buy a pastry, which I'd quickly eaten before I arrived at the library.

Brushing the crumbs from my blouse, I headed onto the library floor, where I slammed into Richard, who I ignored by walking around him.

He came after me.

"Rose, wait. I want to talk to you." He grabbed hold of my arm.

"I have nothing to say to you. Please stop bothering me." I tried to pull my arm free, but he was holding me too tight.

"You're going to regret being with him. He's not worth it. He can't give you what I can."

Anger and frustration filled me and all of it was for Richard. "I will say this for the last time. Leave. Me. Alone." I stomped on his foot, and he released my arm. I hurried away, back to the desk. Mary gave me a quizzical look, but I ignored her and pretended to be sorting through some papers out on the desk. Richard left and I sagged against the desk in relief.

Not long after, Jacob appeared, I followed him behind the antiquated books.

He pulled me straight into his arms and hugged me really tight. I lifted my face for his kiss, and he didn't disappoint me. "I love you. Are you sure about tonight?" he asked.

I took his face in my hands and pulled him down to me. "Yes. I love you and want to spend the rest of my life with you." I kissed him.

"Transport is arranged to get to Boston. Eleanor is really looking forward to having us both living with her."

"I'm so excited, Jacob, but...I need you to come to dinner tonight." He paused with his hand caressing my face. "Richard told my parents about us and what he'd seen. I told my father at breakfast that I love you and plan to marry you. So, my father told me to bring you to dinner tonight."

"Then I'll be there. What time?" he questioned.

"Seven sharp," I whispered, the nerves eating away at me.

"Rose, everything will be fine and, if it isn't, we can still slip away tonight, all right?"

"Yes." I sighed.

We heard voices approaching so he placed a quick peck to my lips and headed out of the library.

How I managed to endure the rest of the day, I would never know. It was such a relief to be on my way home.

I'd just left town when I heard someone shouting my name. I looked behind me...*Richard*. "What do you want now?"

"I'm walking you home, and I plan on staying outside your house all evening to make sure you don't go sneaking off with him."

I glared, shocked. "Have you lost your mind?" He really was crazy.

"No, but you have, for dallying with him."

"I'll have you know that Father has invited Jacob to dinner. So, you see, I don't need to sneak out because he will be eating with me and my family tonight." I stomped off and left him as I reached my house.

I ran upstairs and looked out of the window on the landing only to see Richard still sitting at the end of the drive.

I really couldn't believe he was doing this, to what gain, I had no idea. In my room, I quickly changed into a clean dress, rather than one that was rumpled from a day's work. I brushed my hair and applied my lipstick.

As I ran downstairs, I was in time to watch Jacob walk up the porch steps. I spotted Mother and Father approaching from the parlor, so I ran and opened the door for him. It took all my strength to keep from throwing my arms around his neck.

"Rose." He winked and grinned at me. I felt like melting into a puddle.

"Rose, are you going to invite the young man inside?" my father asked.

"Yes, of course," I replied, grinning at Jacob. I took his hand and pulled him inside, then refused to release him.

"Mother, Father, I would like you to meet Jacob Evans." *Please* let us get through this meal. *Please accept him.*

My parents were polite and shook his hand. Mother stared as we held hands. I loosened my hold slightly, but Jacob tightened his fingers, further intertwining them with mine.

We took our seats in the dining room and all was quiet. Too quiet.

"So, Jacob, Rose was telling us you have been offered an apprenticeship in New York."

With a quick glance at me, he looked back at my father. "Yes, sir, I have. It's with an engineering company. They pay very well."

"Hmm, so what do you intend toward my daughter if you're planning on leaving Cape Elizabeth?"

Jacob placed a hand on my leg underneath the table, knowing I was seconds away from saying something. "Rose has agreed to become my wife, so I'll be taking her with me."

Yes!

"That is enough. You are not going to be marrying my daughter because she is already spoken for." My father's face was red with anger.

I stood and faced my father. "No, I am not, and if you mean Richard, we have already had this discussion."

"I forbid you to spend any more time with this man."

Jacob stood and wrapped his arm around my shoulders, which, with my father in the room, wasn't the wisest thing to do. "Don't worry, Rose. I'm going to leave now, but please don't worry," he whispered into my ear. "I'll go now." He turned to me. "Remember, I love you, Rose." He then walked out of the house, and I ran upstairs to my room, crying.

Although I knew what my father was like, I'd hoped he would accept Jacob, and all would be well. I was stupid to hope.

With my tears dried, I made sure my door was locked and then retrieved another travel bag before I packed my few remaining belongings. I came across the *Our Gang* comic, April 1st edition that I'd bought for JT. Father had refused to let him have it, so I had bought it for him to bribe him to keep quiet.

Taking out the photograph of myself and Jacob, I wrote on the back a small message to JT. I told him I loved him and wished I could take him to Boston with me. I also wrote the address of Jacob's sister, in case he ever needed anything, and I begged him not to tell Mother and Father.

I placed the photograph in the middle of the comic, and then put it to one side, ready to leave on his bed.

Dressed in slacks and a warm sweater for traveling, I climbed onto my bed to rest before it was time for me to leave. I had started to become nervous about the whole thing. I had no doubt whatsoever that I loved Jacob and wanted this baby, his baby, our baby, but it was going to be stressful, doing what I was about to do.

I wondered what to do about my diary. Part of me wanted to take it with me, but another part wanted to leave this part of my life behind. I would have to leave it somewhere safe, where hopefully one day, someone would find it. Part of me hoped it was JT, but the other part hoped it was someone else. I wanted someone to know my story. Maybe they would be inclined to return the diary to me if I was still alive when it was found.

It was ten thirty. I climbed from my bed and collected my purse, bag, and JT's comic, and then slipped quietly out of my room. I went into my brother's room and watched him sleep for a minute before I had to leave. I placed the comic on his bed beside him, as my tears started to flow.

As I walked down the stairs to the kitchen, I'd decided to leave my diary on top of the kitchen cupboards. They were never cleaned so it could be a long time before it was discovered.

And this is where I write my final passage.

Standing at the counter, gazing out at the dark garden beyond the window. Know that I loved you, sweet diary...you were the only confidant I had during all this time. I will miss you dearly but not as dearly as I will miss my JT.

Goodbye, diary.

This is the end of Rose Degan . . . and the beginning of Rose Evans . . .

Chapter 23

I buried my face into Dean's side as my tears flowed freely. I sob as Dean settles me into his arm and gently strokes my back. "It's okay, Mack, let go." And let go I do, while he holds me tight, sobs wracking her body.

Minutes later, I pull slightly away from Dean to search for a tissue, managing to control the waterworks. "Their story is so sad." I start crying again. "She loved him so much, and he obviously loved her. It breaks my heart, knowing that she died that night and Jacob never knew. He always thought she'd left him."

Dean pulls me close once more. "Mack, why not come to see if she'd been held up that night? Why did

Jacob only make one phone call to find out about her? And why did he wait a few days after he left to do it? It doesn't make sense."

I cuddle into his chest, and look up at him, giving a watery smile. "Then let's ask Thomas."

He leans in and kisses my forehead. "What does the J in JT stand for?"

"James."

"Now I really am sure, but it doesn't make sense, why, if he's with another woman, would my grandfather name his firstborn after his lover's brother?"

"What do you mean?'

"My father is James Thomas Evans, and remember, James is my middle name."

I sit up suddenly. "Oh, and then you said your Aunt Rosalind . . ."

"When do you want to see my grandfather?"

I look out to sea and find it hard to get my head around everything. Jacob obviously loved Rose to name his firstborn after Rose's brother, and then his daughter after Rose herself.

"I don't know. I can't really take Lucas, and I don't feel comfortable leaving him all day with Thomas. He can be a real handful."

"Who? Thomas or Lucas?"

"Ha ha…both." I turn back to look at Dean. "Soon. Can I meet him soon?"

He reaches up and moves a piece of hair behind my ear. "Let me know when you're ready and I'll take you."

I take hold of his hand. "Thank you." I place a kiss gently on his knuckles. "So, am I your girl?" I ask with a large grin on my face.

"Yes," he replies without any hesitation. He leans closer and nuzzles my neck. "You are."

"Mmm. Good, because you're my guy." I reach up and run my fingers through his hair, sending shivers down his spine. "I think we'd better head back. I'll ask Thomas about the April 1st edition of *Our Gang*. We can see what he did with the photograph. I would love to see a photograph of Rose and Jacob."

"That would be amazing. We would also know for sure if it's my grandfather. There are photographs all over the house in Brookline from when he was young, so I'll be able to recognize him straightaway."

I MAKE CHICKEN PARMESAN WITH RICE AND I'VE ALSO made two pies, one apple and the other cherry. In fact, I haven't stopped cooking and baking since getting back from the beach. I needed a distraction.

Dean plays one of Lucas's Mario Brothers games in the living room, and apart from him coming back and forth for a beer or munchies, or even delicious kisses, he's pretty much stayed out of the way.

When we read the diary, it had really upset me. I'd cried all over Dean, for heaven's sake. Dean hadn't minded though, he'd held me and tried to comfort me.

My thoughts turn back to Rose. I wonder if Thomas knew about Rose's pregnancy. Did anyone know besides Jacob? Jacob had known Rose was pregnant so wouldn't he have wanted to know about the baby? He seemed to be happy at the prospect of becoming a father. I really need to speak to Jacob to put an end to my wandering mind.

"Auntie Mack, I'm home. Did you miss me?" Lucas practically sings.

I hold my arms out and Lucas runs straight into them. "I sure did, buster. Dean's in there playing Mario."

"Yes!" Lucas darts out of the kitchen to join Dean.

"Hi, Thomas, come sit. Would you like a drink of lemonade?" I ask as he takes a seat at the table.

"That would be mighty fine, thank you."

I pour him a large glass of homemade lemonade. "Can I ask you something?"

He smiles. "You usually do whether I want you to or not."

I place his drink in front of him and sit down on the chair beside him. "Thomas, do you have a photograph of Rose and Jacob together?"

He hesitates. "No, I don't. Never saw one, either."

I'm puzzled. "Are you sure? In her diary, she says that when she was leaving the house, she went into your room and left the April 1st edition of *Our Gang* on your bed. Inside of it, she'd placed a photograph of herself and Jacob with a private message on the back for you?" I trail off at the look on his face.

Thomas looks really shaken. "All this time, I've had a picture of her with him and I didn't even know?"

"I don't understand, Thomas."

He leans forward and puts his arms on the table with his head in his hands. He sighs. "I knew Rose had bought me the comic, and I found it that night, but I didn't get a chance to read it then. When I finally went back to bed, we had been told that Rose had gone over the cliffs so getting into bed, I held the comic and cried. The next morning, I placed it in the box with the others and never opened it. I couldn't."

I take hold of Thomas's hand. "Do you still have it?"

He nods his head. "I took it away from Lucas and placed it on my night table. I intended to finally read it. Maybe it's time. I'll look through it tonight."

"If you find a photograph, will you bring it tomorrow? I'd love to see what Rose looked like, and the man she loved."

He raises his head. "I will."

"Thank you… Rose and Jacob both mean something to me now that I've learned about their love," I admit.

Thomas nods.

"You're staying to eat, right? I've made chicken parmesan and then there's cherry or apple pie with ice cream."

"You do know they say that the way to a man's heart is through his stomach." He chuckles.

"Really? I think I remember something like that." I turn away to check the chicken in the oven, and then turn back to Thomas. "Dean's surname isn't Simone, that's his mother's maiden name."

I have his full attention. "His name is Dean James

Evans, and the James is after his father who Jacob named James Thomas. Dean is Jacob's grandson."

"That's a surprise," Thomas replies, shaking his head.

"Thomas, did you know Rose was pregnant the night she died?"

He takes a deep breath. "Yes. I overheard a conversation between my father and mother after Jacob phoned the house. Apparently, my father had known she was pregnant. I don't know how, but he said he'd told him Rose had lost the baby. He also told my mother that Jacob sounded very shocked. I didn't want you thinking badly of Rose, about her being pregnant, so I didn't tell you when we'd talked before."

I wipe my eyes on the apron I'm wearing. "It's hard to explain, but somehow I feel as though she's talking to me and wants her story told," I wave my arms around, "as ridiculous as that sounds."

We sit lost in our own thoughts for a few minutes. "I know you said Rose had gone over the cliffs, but how, exactly? What happened?" I ask.

"Let me sleep on it, Mack." He shakes his head, looking lost.

I feel guilty having bombarded him with so many questions and brought back painful memories.

I stand with Thomas, give him a hug, which I follow with a kiss to his cheek. "Thank you, Thomas. I don't know about you, but I'm starving. Let's eat."

LYING BACK ON THE SOFA WHILE WAITING FOR MACK to finish getting Lucas in bed, Dean thought about his grandfather.

If everything in Rose's diary was true, and it looked like it was, then why had no one in his family ever mentioned a Rose in his grandfather's past. Why hadn't they mentioned that his grandfather had lived in Cape Elizabeth for a time?

His grandfather had always said he lived his entire life in Boston, apart from the war when he'd been in England. Unless he loved and missed Rose way too much to talk about her.

He had seen wedding photographs of his grandparents, and they'd looked really happy. Dean's father was the eldest and had once told him that his parents were the most loving couple he had ever seen. Even from being a small child, Dean remembered them always holding hands and kissing. He had a really hard time imagining his grandfather like that with anyone but his wife, Eliza.

"You look deep in thought." Mack moved away from the doorway and leaned over the sofa. She looked gorgeous.

"I'm really blown away with everything I've learned today about my grandfather's past. It's unreal."

"I know what you mean. I can't stop now. I need to find out what really happened. It's important to me."

"Is Lucas asleep?"

"Yeah, he was exhausted."

"Come...lie down with me." He held his hand out to her.

She climbed half on top of him, flashing a bit of thigh. Dean caught his breath as he reached out and put his hand on her waist to steady her, only to get a view of her breasts—plump, naked breasts.

He inhaled at the sight of her hovering over him, practically naked. "Mack, you're killing me." He gritted his teeth as he closed his eyes to hide the sight of her so he could gain some control.

When she straddled him, his eyes flew open in time to watch her lose the robe.

"We wouldn't want that now, would we?"

Wouldn't want what? All Dean's brain cells had traveled south, causing his lower body to swell with need. While she was only seconds away from discovering that fact, he couldn't even keep up with the conversation.

"I want your hands and mouth on me, Dean." She leaned over him and softly kissed the tip of his nose, then his eyes, and, finally, she satisfyingly kissed his soft mouth.

Mack broke the kiss, gasping for breath. "You have too many clothes on." She started to pull his T-shirt off, which he ended up yanking over his head and tossing on the floor impatiently.

"You're a goddess," Dean groaned.

She grinned. "You're already getting laid, so you don't need—"

Dean reclaimed her lips while he fondled one small globe, its pink nipple marble hard.

"You set my skin on fire," Mack whispered, kissing down his neck and along his collarbone before moving further south toward his navel, causing a shudder to ripple through Dean.

He gasped. "Stop!"

She froze above him. "Stop?"

"Let me get my jeans off." Breathing heavily, he tried to regain control of his overheated body.

Mack rolled to the side, letting him up, and watched as he removed his clothes in record time. He knelt beside the couch and taking her hand, he guided it to himself, closing his eyes as her fingers wrapped around the full and pulsing length.

Her touch made him crazy and not wanting to embarrass himself, he knocked her hand away and moved over her. He dropped his forehead to Mack's and groaned. "I don't have any protection with me," he admitted. "I'm healthy."

"I'm covered." Mack softly smiled and reaching up, caressed the strong tendons in the back of his neck. "And I'm ready for you... Make love to me."

Dean joined them together, her nipples solid peaks against his hair-roughened chest.

"I've never felt this way before," Dean confessed before he slowly started to love her.

Mack abandoned herself to the whirl of sensation and wrapped herself around him, her hands caressing the planes of his back as the flames of passion burned within them both.

Then minutes later he knew the flooding of uncontrollable joy as she soared to an amazing, shuddering ecstasy.

Dean breathed heavily into her ear when he felt her response to him, and then he lost control and his own body vibrated with liquid fire.

He dropped his head to Mack's shoulder. "I saw stars...the whole universe," he confessed with a kiss to her heated skin.

"Me too," she whispered, sated.

"Let me stay with you tonight. To sleep. I want to hold you in my arms all night."

"Mmm."

Lying on the couch with Mack cuddled in his arms, Dean felt like he was the luckiest man alive.

Over the past week, he'd started to fall in love with her. The thought of her with anyone else caused a deep pain in his chest where his heart was. *Heck! He was in love with her.* He hoped she was in the same place because he had no intention of letting her go.

THOMAS CLIMBED INTO BED FEELING UNSETTLED. Discussing Rose after all these years was rather upsetting, and to discover that she'd left him a photograph with a note on the back... Ah well.

He picked the comic up from his night table and slowly started to turn the pages, holding his breath each time a new page opened. When he turned to the middle of the comic, he found what he was supposed to find seventy years ago, bringing tears to his eyes.

A slightly faded polaroid of his sister Rose, wrapped in the arms of—who he presumed was—Jacob Evans. They both looked so much in love.

Mack had said there was a message on the back for him. He hoped the ink hadn't faded with age. He took a deep breath and turned the picture over to look at the handwriting he never thought he would see again.

Dear JT,

I want you to know that you are the only one I will miss. I love you so much, brother, please forgive me.

If you ever need anything, go to the address at the bottom and ask for Eleanor, she will know how to find me.

When we have our own place and are settled in Boston, I will be back to see

*you. It may take a few years but know
that I will always be thinking about you.
    All my love, Thomas, my JT,
Rose*

He used his fingers to wipe his eyes, and, with shaking hands, he placed the comic and photograph back on the table to the side of his bed. He needed to tell Mack what actually happened that night, and maybe then, he would feel better. After all, he had carried around so much guilt for all these years.

First, though, he would show her the photograph and then think about what to say.

In his eighties, it was time to be free and have peace of mind at last.

Chapter 24

I woke with Dean spooning me tightly from behind, his arm around my waist and a large hand cupped my breast. I felt overwhelmed with contentment.

I can't believe I fell asleep on him last night after the best sex of my life. I hadn't even woken up when he'd obviously carried me upstairs.

"Morning," Dean whispers into my ear, sending shivers down my spine. He smooths his hand down the curve of my waist and hip, then over the top of my thighs.

"Morning." I turn my head for his kiss, and softly smile. "I wish we could stay here all day."

Dean returns my smile. "I do too, but I guess

Lucas is going to be awake soon, so we need to make a move."

"He will be."

Ten minutes later, I towel-dried in the bathroom before I walk back into the bedroom, a towel wrapped around my body. I stop short when I meet Dean's heavy-lidded gaze.

"You're wicked. Look what you've done to me." He lifts the quilt from the top of his hips to show me how affected he is by me.

With a lick of my lips, I look up at the clock and realize Lucas will be up any minute. "Lucas is about to get up, but all I want to do is lick you like a popsicle." I give him a wicked grin.

Dean arches off the bed. "I'm going to have a very cold shower. Please be dressed by the time I get out."

I say, "I'll start breakfast," and grin while watching Dean climb from the bed.

"Even better." He walks past me with a swat on my bottom.

I move downstairs and whistle away while making breakfast. I can't remember ever feeling this way. I've fallen hard for Dean Evans. He always seems to know the right thing to say, or what I need, without me having to say anything. He's easy on the eyes as well, which is an added bonus, and when naked... *Oh boy*!

Thomas walks through the kitchen door, which pulls me from my thoughts of a very naked Dean. "Morning, Mack," he says, but not with his usual flare.

As I look closely at him, I notice how pale he is. "Thomas, are you all right?" I wrap my arms around him. "Come, sit down, and tell me what's wrong. You don't look well. Do you need to go to the doctor?"

"It's not that, Mack," Thomas explains, as Dean comes downstairs.

"Morning, Thomas." Then he sees my concerned expression and pauses. "What's wrong?"

"It's been a very long time since anyone was worried about me. But I'm not sick, just in a little bit of a shock, I guess."

Thomas looks at me. "I found this last night, right where you said it would be." He takes the photograph of Rose and Jacob out of his pocket. He hands it to me, his hands unsteady. I place it face down on the table and sitting down next to him, I take hold of his hands.

"Thank you, Thomas."

"Look at it, Mack, and read what she wrote to me." He has tears in his eyes.

"Auntie Mack, I'm up," Lucas shouts as he comes bouncing into the kitchen. "Thomas… Dean… You're both here… Really early." He pulls up short.

Not knowing what to say, Dean places one of his hands on my shoulder and squeezes. "I'll go and distract him while you talk to Thomas," he whispers.

I press a quick kiss to his palm before letting go. "Thank you."

I watch Dean and Lucas retreat to the living room, no doubt to play some more Super Mario Brothers, which they are both addicted to.

I turn my attention back to Thomas and reach out to pick the photograph up. Turning it over, I take my first look at Rose.

The photograph shows a young couple who are obviously in love with each other. Jacob is taller than Rose, the top of her head only comes to around his shoulders. They are both slim built, although Jacob looks to have some muscle on him, and he has broad shoulders. Rose looks slim and delicate with a ribbon tied around her long blond hair. At least, it looks blond in the black and white photo.

I fight back tears as I look at the photograph. These two were so much in love, and the relationship ended so tragically. It breaks my heart.

I don't feel ready to read what Rose has written, but know I must, for Thomas, and because it will only play on my mind if I don't. I turn the photograph over and finally read what Rose has written to her brother all those years ago.

"Oh, Thomas." I cover my mouth, tears rolling down my face.

"I know, Mack. She really did love me, and if she had made it to Boston, she said she would have come back to see me eventually. Probably when she could stand up to Mother and Father."

I dry my eyes. "Thomas, would you mind if I take a picture with my phone of this photograph?"

"No, that's fine. We'll have to get you a copy made."

"That would be great."

About to snap a copy of the picture, Lucas comes running into the room. Thomas quickly picks the photograph up off the table and puts it back into his pocket.

I pull myself together. "Come on, time for breakfast," I announce, as Dean enters into the kitchen.

He moves over to me and runs his hand down my back in a loving caress. "Are you okay?" he whisper before placing a sweet kiss to my lips.

"I am now," I reply, grinning. "Come on, Dean. Let's eat."

Breakfast is a silent affair, each of us lost in our own thoughts.

"You're looking mighty happy with yourself, young man," Thomas says, pointing his fork at Dean, which draws my attention to his handsome face.

"Um, yes I am," he replies while eating his breakfast.

"Are you going to share?" Thomas looks back and forth between Dean and myself.

"I might share my thoughts, but I'm not sharing my woman," Dean says to a laughing Thomas across the table.

"Who's your woman?" Lucas pipes up.

Dean pauses with the last of his breakfast about to disappear into his mouth. "Your Auntie Mack. Is that all right with you, Lucas?"

"If you make her cry, I'm going to beat you up," Lucas growls.

Dean's expression turns serious as he says, "If I make her cry, I'll let you beat me up. Is that a deal?" He holds out his hand to Lucas, who looks at it then shakes it with sticky fingers.

"Deal."

"Don't I get a say in any of this?" I ask.

Lucas and Dean both look my way. "No!" they say together.

I laugh. "Okay, if all the macho stuff is out of the way, what's everyone doing today?"

"I'm going drinking with Thomas," Lucas informs us with glee.

"Oh, you are, are you?" I raise an eyebrow in Thomas's direction and wait for an explanation, which isn't long in coming.

"Well now, I usually meet a couple of old friends every week, and today is the day. We play cards, and people watch. They want me to bring Lucas as I mentioned him a time or two the other night."

I frown, not sure it wise to give Lucas freedom around three elder men. "Are you sure Lucas will be okay there?"

"Don't be worrying. You have enough on your plate right now. Lucas will be fine. If I didn't think he would be, I wouldn't take him."

"Okay, but I'll pick him up just after lunch."

Lucas starts jumping up and down. "Yes, yes, yes, I'm going drinking. I'm going drinking." He dances around the kitchen.

I drop my head into my hands, groaning. Dean and Thomas roar with laughter.

"Lucas. Do not, under any condition, tell your father."

"Why, Auntie Mack? Daddy always says you have to at least do everything once."

I glance at Thomas and Dean then give them a dirty look because they are still laughing. "Lucas, I don't think your daddy meant for you to do it all while you're still six."

"Okay, scout's honor, this is our secret. I'm going up to wash my hands. Back in a minute, Thomas." Lucas rushes off.

"You do realize as soon as he sees his father that this adventure will be the first thing, he tells him?" I pick up my coffee and take a sip while thinking about Lucas's trip with Thomas. Hopefully, he won't get into too much trouble.

"Spend today with me again?" Dean asks, breaking into my thoughts.

"I'd love to."

"Well, who do we have here, Thomas?"

"This is my good friend, Lucas Cartwright. Lucas, meet a couple of friends of mine, Levi, and Walt. We've been friends for seventy-seven years."

Lucas's jaw dropped and Levi smiled. "Well, come on over here and tell us some gossip, kid."

He took a seat between Levi and Thomas. "What do you want to know?"

"Well now, let me think. What's going on up at that cottage of Thomas's that you're staying in?"

"Oh, that's easy. My auntie has a secret about something she found about someone named Rose, and Dean slept in her bed last night, but she doesn't know I know that. Is that what you mean?" Lucas looked at the stunned faces looking back at him. "What did I say?"

Thomas came back to his wits first. "You did fine, Lucas. Why don't I teach you how to play poker so you can fleece your father," he replied, trying to change the subject.

"That would be cool." Lucas grinned.

Thomas hadn't expected that kind of gossip to come out of Lucas's mouth. He was a handful all right. He chuckled to himself.

Tomorrow.

Tomorrow, he would talk to Mack about the night Rose died. Maybe. Maybe not.

Thomas glanced quickly over at Levi and Walt, who still seemed a little bit preoccupied. He guessed they were thinking back to the time Rose died.

"Let's shuffle the cards."

"DEAN, DO YOU THINK THE LIBRARY HERE IN TOWN WILL have newspaper archives from 1947?" I move to sit beside him on the sofa.

He reaches out and pulls me toward him. "Probably, why? What are you thinking?"

"I'm thinking that if Thomas can't talk, then surely there would have been something about a young woman going off the cliffs written up in the newspaper. If there was, why didn't Jacob read about it? Most people read newspapers, more so back then, I would have thought."

"You've got a point. Do you want to go?"

I sit up to look closely at him. "Are you sure you don't mind spending time at the library?"

"As long as I'm with you, I don't mind." He caresses my face then leans in to kiss me.

As he pulls away, I lay my palms against his face and pull him down so that I can reach his lips for a quick kiss. "Mmm." I lick my lips. "Thank you for being understanding. I really appreciate it. We could go somewhere after the library if you'd like."

"I'd like."

"Oh, I almost forgot. I took a picture of the photograph Thomas found. Let me show you."

Reaching for my phone, I open the photograph app and click on the image I took. Unfortunately, it's a really bad copy and doesn't really show the faces. I must have taken the picture as Thomas removed it from the table when Lucas appeared.

"Damn, this is totally rubbish. Look." I pass my phone to Dean.

"You can take another one, Mack. In fact, when we go to visit my grandfather, I'll bring my laptop and portable scanner back here, and we can get a better copy for you." Dean stands and grabs his jacket from the back of the kitchen chair.

I follow him out of the cottage. "That would be great. Thanks."

He puts his arm around my neck and brings me in close before he places a soft kiss on the top of my head. "Come on, the library awaits," he says.

It only takes ten minutes before Dean pulls his bike into a parking space outside of the library while I wonder if it's the same library where Rose had worked all those years ago. Parts of it certainly look old enough, although it look like new sections have been added over time.

We climb off Dean's bike and remove our helmets. I reach up and pull his head down to mine for a slow kiss, and then once I pull away, I give him a flirtatious look.

"What was that for?" He wraps his arms around me and pulls me even closer to nuzzle into my neck.

"I can't resist you." I groan.

A car suddenly backfires, which brings us back to our senses. I take a deep breath and move away. "We'd better head inside."

I giggle when I catch the look on Dean's face. We are acting like lovesick teenagers. I open the door to the library and stand with my hands on my hips, waiting for him to catch up.

He ushers me inside, laughing.

The library is large as I glance around the sturdy bookshelves that line the walls, marching across the floor in rows, curling around reading nooks and study areas. A long front desk manned by librarians and their assistants looks busy for a small town.

An assistant directs us to the relevant section, telling us to come find him if we need any help.

Dean joins me and reaching for me, pulls me in for a quick kiss. "He wanted you," he mutters.

I frown. "Who? The assistant?"

Dean glares.

"Well, I'm taken." I move away. "The newspapers we want are over here. Apparently, each page is laminated for protection, so he didn't have any problem leaving us alone in here." I look back at Dean.

"Alone? For how long?"

I laugh. "Come over here and help. You're taller than me."

"Yes, ma'am." He saunters over, laughing.

He lifts the volume down that covers the week of April 14, 1947, and sets it down on the table, while I take my jacket off and place it on top of his on the chair.

I'm really excited, hoping there is something in these papers about what happened to Rose. It appears to have been awhile since anyone has looked through them because they are caked in a few layers of dust. I blow it off the best I can, then turn the page to April

15th. We eagerly scan each page closely to try to find something.

As we carefully look through the 19th, I start to lose hope of finding anything. It's five days after the event, and surely, it will have been covered before then.

As I start to turn the page, something catches Dean's eye. He places his hand out and stops the page from turning. "Mack, look. Read this."

April 19, 1947

Today the Coast Guard called off the search for the missing person who was witnessed falling to their death over the cliffs on the evening of the 14th. Female clothing has come ashore on the beach, but as of yet, there is still no sign of a body.

If anyone has any information about the identity of the missing person, presumed female, please contact . . .

"Could this be Rose?" I lift my eyes to look at Dean, excitement filling me gaze.

He pulls me out of the chair and onto his lap. "I

don't know. It sounds like it. But why isn't her name in the article? It's as though no one knows it's Rose."

I snuggle into him. "I'm going to have to ask Thomas. It doesn't make sense. Her family obviously had money. If her father was trying to marry her off to a wealthy guy, her drowning should have been bigger news."

"Come on, let's go and get something to eat, then head back and see if there's anything out there on the internet about Rose. There should at least be a death certificate we can view."

"IT'S AUNTIE MACK AND DEAN." LUCAS SHOOTS UP out of his chair and runs straight into my arms.

"Are you okay, Lucas?" I ask as Dean walks in, ruffling Lucas' hair.

"Yes." He moves and sits down to finish his lunch.

Thomas wipes his mouth with a napkin with a soft smile on his face as he gazes at Lucas, who is busy arranging his remaining fries into a row of soldiers on this place. Lucas then shovels more ketchup-covered fries into his mouth. "I can play poker," Lucas adds with great pride.

"Oh, you can, can you?" I grin at Dean.

"Mack, Dean," Thomas says, "I'd like you to meet Levi."

"What? You're Levi. I mean, *Levi*?" I laugh. "Sorry, I'm not usually an idiot. I mean Levi as in the childhood friend of Thomas?" I find it unbelievable that Levi and Thomas are still best friends after all these years.

Dean hands me an ice-cold Pepsi and puts his down on the table. He carries a couple of chairs over for us. Placing both chairs close together, he eases me down into one. He gives my shoulder a squeeze and whispers in my ear, "What's wrong?"

I turn to reply and stop when I realize how close to Dean's face I am. Looking into his eyes, I lean forward slightly. "I'm okay." Then I kiss him.

I move slightly away and notice a twinkle in Thomas's eye. *He probably has us married already*, I think. After I've taken a long drink of the Pepsi, I look over at Thomas. "How long have you known Levi?"

"Seventy-seven years, or thereabouts."

"Damn, that's a long time," Dean mutters.

"In Rose's diary, she mentioned you a couple of times. In fact, the description that really made me laugh was about you and Thomas running off with an apple pie, and that you both got caught returning the plate."

"I remember that as though it was yesterday," Levi replies laughing.

"Levi, can I ask you something?"

He pauses, and taking a sip of his drink, he quickly glances at Thomas. "Yes, I guess. As long as it isn't going to get me into trouble."

Dean reaches down and removes my hand from his thigh. He laced our fingers together.

"Do you remember Rose? What she was like?"

"I do." He has a slight blush. "She was the most beautiful girl I'd ever seen, and I had a crush on her. I didn't tell Thomas, but I had planned on marrying her when I was ten."

"I knew." Thomas laughs.

"What's a crush?" Lucas asks, having finished his huge, ice cream sundae.

"A crush is when you really like someone, and you can't think about anyone else," I reply to Lucas, who still looks confused.

"So, you mean like you and Dean?"

"Yes, like me and your Auntie Mack," Dean answers, grinning at me.

Dean's phone starts to ring. "Excuse me a minute. It's my mother." He stands, and before he walks outside to answer the call, places a quick kiss on the top of my head.

My sandwich arrives but I keep glancing outside to catch a glimpse of Dean. Wherever he is, my eyes are always drawn to him. Is this how Rose felt when she was with Jacob?

Dean comes back inside and appears rather distracted as he sits back down. "Is everything okay? You look bothered."

He sighs in frustration. "I'm fine." Then he holds my gaze. "I have to go to Boston tomorrow for a garden party at my folks' place. Do you and Lucas want to go with me? We would, of course, have to go in your car, but we could share the driving. We could also bring my laptop and scanner back as well."

I stay silent, not sure whether it's a good idea to meet his family after only knowing each other for a short time.

"Mack?" he asks nervously.

"Are you sure you want me to meet your family?" I whisper.

Dean takes hold of my hands. "Yes, I do. I need to

warn you, though, Cynthia, who I mentioned before, will be there trying to get her claws into me...you know...maybe this isn't a good idea, after all."

I hear Dean say Cynthia is going to be there and feel my hackles rise at the woman's name. There is no way my man is going to a party without me when another woman wants him. No way in hell.

"Yes, we would love to go," I reply and notice a mixture of relief and fright cross Dean's face. I giggle. "I'll sharpen my knives. No one messes with my guy."

"You're hot when you're being protective, and honey, I'm all yours," Dean whispers into my ear.

Thomas stands, and taking hold of Lucas's hand, says, "We're going to the beach for the afternoon, so I'll have the boy back home for dinner."

"Are you sure, Thomas?" I'm worried about leaving Lucas all day with him. I'm supposed to be the one spending all my time with him.

"I'm sure... I'm not about to miss dinner," Thomas says while I grin at his cheek.

We finish our lunch in silence as we watch Thomas and Levi take Lucas across the road to the shady part of the beach. For the second time, I wonder what it would be like to live in Cape Elizabeth instead of the city.

"You finished?" Dean asks rather abruptly.

"I am, thanks. That was really good." I wipe my mouth on a napkin while I watch Dean place the dishes onto the bar and let my mind wander back to last night and how he'd looked.

Dean starts to head back and notices the way my eyes rove over him. He hesitates. "What do you want to do now?"

I lick my lips and stand. "Mmm, how about going back to my place?" I wiggle my brows.

Dean tightens his hold on his jacket, picks the helmets up, and then practically drags me out of the door.

Not ten minutes later, I lead Dean into the cottage, enjoying watching him prowl toward me as I perch on the edge of the kitchen table and smirk while I slowly unfasten the top button of my shirt. "Love me," I whisper.

The minute I unfasten my jeans, Dean rips his T-shirt over his head, and his lips meet mine in a fiery kiss that sends currents of desire racing through me. He grasps my bottom in his big hands and pulls me against his arousal that throbs behind his zipper.

Dean pushes me slightly away to unhook my bra, and as he eases the cups away, he hisses at the sight.

He places a teasing kiss to one of my rose-colored nipples while my hands run along the planes of his back. The heat and lust between us drives my desire higher especially when his mouth latches around a nipple. He sucks and plays with the hardening bud with his delicious tongue.

"Dean," I groan, frantic.

He pushes me back so that I'm lying on the table as he watches my breasts heave, my nipples red and swollen from his mouth. He makes quick work of my jeans and panties. As soon as I'm free of clothing, I wrap my legs around his hips and rub myself on him.

Dean pants. "You drive me totally crazy. You know that Mack?"

I moan. "Dean, now!" I grab hold of Dean's arm and pull myself up. I unzip his jeans, push them down past his hips and take hold of his erection, which pulses and weeps in my hands.

"Christ, Mack." He moves my hands away and crushes his lips against mine. He grabs my hips with his trembling hands, moves me to the edge of the table, and thrusts inside.

I gasp and watch his reaction as I clench around his shaft, smiling when his eyes roll back in pleasure.

DEAN COMES UP BEHIND ME IN THE KITCHEN AS I STIR the sauce in a pan, wrapping his arms around my midriff, my heart flutters. He places kisses along my neck. "Mmm, you taste good."

I smile up at him, quickly kiss him, and then push him slightly away. "Thomas and Lucas are here."

"What have you been doing while we were at the beach?" Lucas asks, which makes me blush and I catch Dean smiling.

"I've been cooking, and Dean has been trying to beat his score on that game you both seem to like."

"Cool." Lucas heads into the living room to check out Dean's latest score.

"Thomas, can I ask you something about Rose, please?" Dean asks, which draws both mine and Thomas's attention.

"I guess." Sitting down, Thomas looks apprehensive.

"Why isn't Rose's name in the newspapers about her disappearance?" Thomas raises his head, as Dean continues, "It says in the paper 'missing person,' and they also ask for anyone to come forward if they know the identity of that person. We visited the library archives this morning."

Thomas lets out a long slow sigh. "It was Rose. Richard, who wanted to marry her, was the son of the paper's owner at the time. My father had a word with him, and although something had to be printed, they made sure it was very small and with no names."

I shoot a quick glance to Dean.

"Looking back now, I guess they could have done that so Jacob, if reading a paper, wouldn't have a clue it was Rose. Why? I don't know. Perhaps they blamed him and thought he would suffer more anguish thinking she didn't love him and had chosen Richard instead of letting him know that she'd died," Thomas says.

"That is sad. Did they ever find her?" I ask.

Tears sting Thomas's eyes. "No."

I take hold of Thomas's hands while Dean puts his arm around my shoulders. "I'm so sorry, Thomas," I say, crying with him and for him.

"Don't worry. It was a long time ago. It's hard reliving it." He pats my hand.

"I'm not helping, am I?" I wipe my tears away.

"It's time I got everything off my chest. I'm feeling

weary tonight, but maybe tomorrow." He smiles softly.

I squeeze Thomas's hand in thanks and while I'm lost in my own thoughts, Dean is inviting Thomas to go with us to the garden party tomorrow, much to Lucas's delight.

Chapter 25

THE GARDEN PARTY HAD BEEN CANCELLED, SO WE'D spent the day on the beach with Thomas yesterday. We'd swam. We picnicked. We napped. It was such a fun day.

Before Lucas awakened for the day, Dean had left to go back to his cottage, and is expected back shortly for breakfast, along with Thomas.

Hearing rustling at the back door, I turn in time to watch Thomas walk in with another bunch of flowers.

"For a beautiful woman." Thomas holds out a lovely bunch of carnations.

I take the flowers from him. "They're lovely.

You're already in my heart, you know, and I'll still feed you, even if you run out of flowers."

He winks. "I'll never run out of flowers for you."

"Are you trying to steal my woman again?" Dean asks as he enters the kitchen, going straight over to me laughing. He plants a possessive kiss on my lips, then asked, "Where's Lucas?"

"Living room."

Dean disappears, no doubt to play a game with Lucas for a short while.

I start to stack the pancakes, leaving Thomas to get lost in thoughts of his own.

"After breakfast, do you think we could talk? I need to tell you what happened that night."

Thomas has taken me by surprise. I'd hoped that he would talk to me about the night Rose died, but I hadn't been expecting him to be ready yet.

"Thank you, Thomas. I know after all this time that it still isn't easy for you to talk about."

Thomas nods his head in acknowledgment as he takes his seat at the table.

With apprehension settling in the pit of my stomach about what I will discover later, I shout for Dean and Lucas to come into the kitchen for breakfast.

Once everyone has washed up, we sit to eat the feast I've made.

I turn to Dean. "Would you mind keeping an eye on Lucas while I talk to Thomas after breakfast?"

Dean grins across to Lucas. "That won't be a problem."

"Why do you need to talk to Thomas?" Lucas asks, reaching for a slice of bacon.

"You know about the diary I've been reading?" I question, knowing that he's discovered what I've been hiding.

"You mean the one you are hiding from me." Lucas grins. "Yes, I know about that."

I chuckle. "Well, it was written by Thomas's sister, Rose, and Thomas is going to tell me more about her."

Lucas is thoughtful and then nods. "Okay. Can you pass me the syrup please?"

I blink at his rapid change of subject and pass him the syrup. "You'll have fun with Dean."

"DEAN."

"Yes, Lucas." Dean wondered what was on his young mind.

"Are you going to marry Auntie Mack? Because that will make you, my uncle."

Dean didn't really know how to answer. "Would it bother you if I did?"

"No. I like you and wouldn't mind having an uncle. Thomas has already said he will be my other granddad."

He laughed. "It doesn't always work like that Lucas, but I'll tell you a secret." Lucas moved closer to Dean as he whispered into Lucas's ear. "I love your Auntie Mack, and I hope to be around her a very, very long time. Will that do for now?"

"As long as you remember it's my birthday soon, and there's a new Mario Brothers game coming out, so if you are my uncle, you have to buy me a present."

He ruffled Lucas's hair. "I'll remember that. Now, are you going to let me win this one?"

"No way!"

Halfway through the first game, Dean realized that Lucas excelled at not only the game, but at the coordination needed for it, and the way his young mind worked to get himself free of the dungeon surprised him. He knew that games could teach as well as distract, after all it had been an online program that had gotten him through math's while at college. Just the thought of the dreaded subject made him shudder. To this day he had no clue why he even chose it as a minor.

WHEN WE ARRIVE AT THOMAS'S COTTAGE, I LOOK across at him, noticing that he looks really frail, and for maybe the first time, he looks his age.

"Thomas, are you sure you're okay doing this? You look awfully pale," I ask, concerned.

"I'm fine, Mack. Collecting my thoughts so they don't come out all jumbled."

We enter through the porch, and I notice how neat and tidy everywhere is. Nothing like my apartment in Boston.

"Let's go to the living room, Mack. It's comfortable in there."

"Lead the way."

I take a seat in the living room and look around, spotting all the photographs on the sideboard. Thomas notices me looking. "Those are pictures of my wife and various friends over the years."

I stand and walk over to take a closer look at the photographs of Thomas's life. I pick up the photograph of Rose and Jacob, which he has already framed and placed in the center of the pictures. There is a photograph of Thomas on his wedding day with his beautiful bride.

He notices the photograph that has sparked my interest. "That's Janet and me on our wedding day in 1958. She was the most beautiful woman I'd ever seen. Couldn't believe it when she showed interest in me." He laughs. "After our first date, we were pretty much inseparable and married three months later."

"These are amazing, Thomas. Oh, is that you?" I pick up a photograph of what looks to be a younger Thomas in uniform.

"That's me. I joined the army as soon as I was old enough. Against my father's wishes, I might add. He never spoke to me again after I became a soldier."

I felt angry on Thomas's behalf. "I wish he was here now so I could give him a piece of my mind."

"Don't worry, Mack. It was a long time ago. In fact, that picture was taken before I shipped out to Korea in 1953."

"Wow."

"Come sit next to me, Mack. Let me tell you a story."

"I'm all yours, Thomas."

"It might disappoint you some as my reluctance to talk is more about guilt, than anything else."

"Thomas don't worry. Tell me anything that you can remember."

"I remember that last night as though it happened yesterday... It was after ten thirty when I woke up, having heard my bedroom door shut. Turning over, I heard a thump, so I climbed out of my bed and turned on the lamp in my room. I discovered the *Our Gang*, April 1st edition on the floor. I realized it must have been Rose who had been in my room."

He sighs. "I then put the comic down on my bed and put on my slippers and a sweater before creeping downstairs. Spotting a light in the kitchen, I slipped inside quietly, and saw her going out the door with her purse."

He takes a sip of water. "I knew she was going to meet, Jacob, but I had no idea she had planned to run away with him. At least not then. It must have been about five minutes later, when Richard came banging on the back door. He had seen Rose sneak out and wanted to know where she was going. I told him I had no idea. He frightened me. I ended up blurting out that I thought she'd snuck out to meet Jacob and she would probably take the cliff path toward town."

We have tears in our eyes, when I ask Thomas, "Are you sure you're okay to continue?"

"I haven't spoken about that night before now. I need to tell you." He nods, trying to convince himself.

"All right, go on."

"Richard seemed to go wild when I explained. He said, 'I will find her and bring her back where she belongs, and that is as my wife.' I have never forgotten those words. Richard then took off toward the cliffs and that was the last I saw of him, until he returned over an hour later, when Mother and Father were home, and told them he saw her go over the cliffs. I remember Richard looking really upset and as he was telling us, he crumpled, breaking down sobbing."

"Oh, Thomas." I kneel at his feet, taking his hands into mine. "Did you believe Richard when he said she'd *fallen* off the cliff, or did you consider Richard might have pushed her off?"

"I don't know, Mack. That was a possibility, and I guess that night Richard looked wild enough to do anything, but he never, in all the years before that night or following, showed any sign of being dangerous. Plus, I think he really did love her. He seemed a gentle kind of guy. At least, that's what I thought."

I sit upright. "Thomas, is Richard still alive?"

"He is, Mack. He lives in a nursing home in Portland now that he needs round-the-clock care."

"Do you think they would let me talk to him?"

"He has a daughter, Sally. She works in town at the market on Ocean House Road. You could go see her and maybe she could help you."

"Over the years, have you ever asked Richard what happened that night?" I asked him tentatively.

"I tried, when I was older, maybe ten years later. He said that he'd lost the only woman he'd ever loved that night and didn't want to remember. Then he walked away from me."

"I don't know what to say. But I do know more happened that night than what you were told, I'm sure of it. I'm going to find out what. Perhaps now that Richard isn't doing so well, he may be more open to talking about what happened that night, providing he remembers."

Thomas pulls himself together and looks across to me. "Thank you. I feel as though a weight has been lifted from my shoulders. I've always blamed myself, you see, for not telling my father. If I had, he probably would have done his best to split them up but, at least, she would've lived. It was my fault Richard went after her on the cliff path."

"You don't know that. Please don't blame yourself anymore. It wasn't your fault. I'm glad you told me, and I'll let you know how my visit to see Richard goes," I explain.

"Take Dean with you when you go, Mack. He might need round-the-clock care, but I don't want you alone with him."

I glance at Thomas. "I will do... Do you want to come back with me for some lunch?"

"No, thank you. I think I need some peace for a short time. I'll see you for dinner though."

When I leave Thomas, I realize that I still have many unanswered questions.

Chapter 26

AFTER SPEAKING WITH SALLY, RICHARD'S DAUGHTER, we're driving to Richard's nursing home. I watch the countryside fly past with nerves in my belly while I ponder what Richard might tell us. It's so long ago, which makes me wonder just what Richard will remember from that time, if anything.

With a heavy sigh, I rest against the back of the seat and watch Dean as he concentrates on the road. I am so in love with him and have no idea what is going to happen at the end of the summer. However, I have a gut feeling Dean is with me for much longer than the summer.

Lucas is staying with Thomas and Levi in the bar until after lunch to give us a couple of hours. I hope

Lucas behaves himself, and with a bit of luck, keeps his thoughts to himself for a change.

"We're here, Mack." Dean pulls into a parking space at the home.

I stare out of the window and survey the scene as Dean walks around to open my door.

Resting his arms on the side of the car, he asks, "You ready to do this?"

"No, not really. Do you think I'm doing the right thing?" I'm terrified of what Richard might reveal.

"You have to do this. If you don't, you'll always wonder."

I let Dean pull me out of the car and take hold of his hand as we walk toward the entrance.

Inside we are greeted by a nurse, who asks us the name of the person we are there to visit.

I reply, "Richard," then it suddenly dawns on me that I don't know his surname. I blush fiercely trying to recall it, but I don't think Rose had written it down… Thomas had certainly never told me. When I mention Sally, we are pointed to the correct room.

On entering Richard's room, we find it rather dark, and there are two small lamps switched on, although it does little to illuminate the small room with their soft, orange glow.

"I can't see you over there," a rough voice grumbles.

I move forward, my hand still held tightly by Dean and take a seat to the side of the bed.

"Hello, Richard. My name is Mackenzie Harper, and this is a good friend of mine, Dean...Simone. We're sorry to disturb you, but we were wondering if you would be willing to talk to us about something that happened a long time ago?" I hold my breath while I wait anxiously for Richard's reply. He takes so long to answer that I start to fidget. Dean tightens his hold on my hand in reassurance.

"Do I make you nervous, young lady?"

I hesitate. "Actually, yes, you do. I'm nervous about asking you what it is I need to know."

"So, ask me and get it out of the way."

I inhale deeply. "I found a diary dated 1947, it belonged to Rose Degan."

Richard inadvertently stills. His eyes narrow.

"You remember Rose, don't you, Richard?"

After a few moments, he focuses on me. "Rose was the first woman I ever loved, and I never loved anyone else like I did her. She was everything to me," his voice breaks.

"Will you tell us what happened the night she died? Please, Richard?"

He doesn't answer but instead looks toward the curtained window as if he is seeing something else. Finally, he looks back at us and whispers, "I've never spoken about that night since it happened, and then I only said I saw her go over the cliffs from a distance."

"What really happened that night?"

He sighs heavily as he closes his eyes, and then he slowly starts talking, "I stayed outside that night after she got home from work. I was so jealous, and I wanted to make sure she didn't sneak out to meet him. I'd taken sandwiches to eat for dinner and a thermos of coffee. Unbeknown to me, Jacob had been invited to dinner by her father. Don't know what happened, but he left soon after arriving. So, I stayed, knowing deep down that she would try to sneak out to see him. Later, I don't know what time it was, I saw a figure moving quickly away from the house. I knew instinctively it was Rose, so I ran in the same direction and then she disappeared from sight."

Richard opens his eyes and stares at me. "I'm not proud of what I did next, but I loved her, and I panicked."

"We're not here to judge you, Richard. We want to know what happened to Rose."

Richard takes a deep, rattling, breath. "I went running to the back door and started banging on it. I wanted to tell Rose's father that she was gone, but Thomas opened it. He looked upset himself. I threatened him so that he would tell me where she had gone." He pauses and shakes his head. "He told me he thought she had gone to meet Jacob, and that she normally took the footpath over the cliffs."

Richard looks distressed so I stand and move to help him take a few sips of water.

"Thank you."

He doesn't look too good. "Richard, do you want to continue?"

"Yes. It's about time I admitted the truth."

"Okay," I say, hesitantly. I want the truth, but a part of me is terrified at what he will say. I take my next to Dean.

"I'd caught up to Rose at the cliffs. She was standing there, near the edge, lost in her own thoughts. I made her jump in surprise." He coughs. "She turned around to look at me and wanted to know what I was doing there. I told her I loved her and wanted her to stay with me and marry me. She laughed in my face. Rose told me that she was in love with Jacob, and only him, and that she was," he wipes tears from his eyes, "pregnant with Jacob's child. She told me that she was running away to marry him. I begged her not to. I told her that I would still marry her, and we could raise the child as mine. She told me no, and as I started very slowly walking toward her, she took a couple of steps back, and went off the cliffs."

Richard stops and gulps in some much-needed air. "After that, I went back to Degan House. Her parents had arrived home by then. I told them that I saw her go over the cliffs from a distance and that I never had a chance to talk to her." He pauses. "About a week later, her father came to see me and asked what had really happened. I told him about the baby. He was angry and ended up punching me. He told me never to talk about Rose again. I really did love her, Mackenzie. I didn't mean for her to fall, and I would have saved her if I could have."

As Richard finishes talking, I hand him a tissue. I take one for myself and look at Dean, who also has tears in his eyes. I turn and hug him tightly.

I look at Richard. "Thank you for telling us. It means a lot."

"Tell Thomas I'm sorry for not saying any of this way back then. I was in shock and," he pauses, "a coward. I'm not proud of my actions. I thought everyone would think I'd pushed her off because she was going to him instead of choosing me."

"Oh!" I have to take some deep breaths so I don't start crying.

"I need to rest now," Richard says, his lips turning into a scowl as his hands begin to shake in agitation. He dismisses us with one sweep of his old, wrinkled hand.

Dean takes hold of my hand and leads me back to the car. He helps me inside before he runs around the front to climb in himself. "Where do you want to go from here, Mack?"

I offer him a sad smile. "Home."

"Okay. Anything you say."

BACK AT ROSE COTTAGE, DEAN USHERS ME INSIDE AND into a chair at the kitchen table. "Your hands are freezing." He turns to warm some water for a hot drink, trying to bring some life back into me.

With a drink made, he passes it to me and wraps

my fingers gently around the warm cup. "Thank you, Dean, for being there with me."

He moves his chair closer to mine as he puts an arm around me and rubs my shoulder with his hand. "I'm here for you...now and always. I love you and I'm not going anywhere." He cups his hand underneath my chin and tips my face up to his for a sweet, slow kiss.

"Are you sure, Dean?"

Dean smiles. "Yes, Mack. I am. If that's okay with you?"

"Mmm. That's more than okay."

The next minute, Lucas barges right through the kitchen door. "Auntie Mack, you're back." Not realizing he's interrupted anything, Lucas carries on walking straight through to the living room. "You coming, Dean?" he shouts, his voice filled with challenge.

Dean glances at me. "In a minute, champ." He stands and tugs me up and into his arms. I wrap my arms tightly around his waist and enjoy the feel of him as I slip my hands into the back pocket of his jeans.

He chuckles and leaning closer, captures my lips

with his. Breathing heavily, he whispers, "You're asking for trouble by doing that."

"Promises, promises." I laugh.

About to grab me again, Dean stops himself as Thomas walks through the back door.

"Are you feeling better, Mack?" Dean asks.

I nod.

Dean smiles. "We'll finish what *you* started later," he whispers, and plants a quick kiss on my lips before he joins Lucas in the living room.

Thomas walks cautiously into the room before he makes eye contact with me.

I smile. "Thomas, we spoke to Richard this morning." I take a seat at the table and wait for Thomas to join me. "He told me what happened that night, and he also told me how your father knew Rose was pregnant."

Thomas silently rubs his face with his hands. "I did wonder if Richard had spoken to her before she'd died because I could never figure out how Father knew she was pregnant."

"Apparently, he found her at the cliffs and begged her to stay and marry him. He said she's the only woman he has ever loved, and I believe him. Richard told Rose he would even bring Jacob's child up as his own."

He shakes his head. "He was married and has a daughter. Are you saying he admitted to only loving my sister, Rose?"

"No. He said she was the first woman he had ever loved, and he never loved anyone else as much. I guess he loved his wife, but in a different way."

"Then I feel sorry for him. His wife was a lovely woman. In fact, she was best friends with my wife, and when Janet died, she would bring meals to me three times a week."

I sit quietly for a short time, at a loss for words. "Richard said to tell you that he was sorry he never told you anything about that night. He presumed everyone would think that he'd pushed her over because she'd chosen Jacob instead of him."

I glance into the living room to make sure Dean has Lucas occupied. I catch Dean's eyes. He winks and blows me a kiss, which makes my heart flutter.

Thomas takes hold of my hand and squeezes. "Thank you... I guess, in the back of my mind, I've always wondered whether or not he had anything to do with her death. I can't imagine what he must have felt like, watching the woman he loved go over the cliffs."

"It's all so sad. Dean is going to arrange for me to meet his grandfather soon. I'm not looking forward to telling him, but he needs to know, and I really need to be the one to tell him. I feel connected to Rose. Their story breaks my heart."

Dean and Lucas appear.

"Auntie Mack, after dinner can I go and have a sleepover at Thomas's cottage…please?"

I glance at Thomas, who is nodding his head. "Are you sure, Thomas?"

Thomas looks choked up. "I'd love that, I really would."

I look at an excited Lucas. "Well then, I guess we better pack you a bag." He runs upstairs.

"My sister called." I sigh, not wanting to tell Thomas this, "They're collecting Lucas tomorrow and taking him to Florida. A visit with Mickey Mouse."

"He'll love that." Thomas squeezes my shoulder and leaves.

Chapter 27

THOMAS HADN'T SHOWED UP FOR BREAKFAST, SO WE had called to check on him before heading out to Boston. We discovered him well, although a bit down, with Lucas having departed for Florida the night before.

Once again, I'm left to my own thoughts, wondering how Jacob will react to what I have to say. It has been a long time since his love affair with Rose, but I would bet anything that he remembers Rose as though it was yesterday. You don't forget a love like they obviously had, especially with it ending like it did.

With everything going on, I've forgotten to get

another copy of the photograph of Rose and Jacob, which is unbelievable, considering how obsessed I am with them.

All too soon, Dean brings the car to a stop in front of his family's home and turns to look at me. "Are you ready to do this? I have to admit, I'm nervous, so I can't imagine what you're feeling."

"I'm nervous, and excited, to be finally meeting him. Not just because of Rose, but because he's your grandfather."

Dean climbs out of the car and walks around to help me out. He places a kiss to my lips before he captures my hand and pulls me toward the house. "Come on."

We enter the house and are met by Martha, his grandparents' housekeeper, who looks down at our joined hands and back up at our faces. "Mr. Dean, I didn't know you were coming home."

"I'm not, Martha, this is Mack. We're here to visit my grandparents. Where are they?"

"Your grandfather is in the study, and your grand-mother went to the…powder room."

"Okay, thanks." He turns to me and pulls me toward his grandfather's study. "I'll go in and introduce you, and then I'll go and distract my grandmother."

"Okay."

"It'll be all right." Dean gives me a quick kiss.

He knocks on the study door, and then walks in, dragging a partly reluctant me behind him.

"Dean, my boy, where have you been?" his grandfather asks while he hugs Dean with obvious affection.

I get a better look at him. He's a distinguished older man with grey hair and, despite his age, is still well built with a very slight paunch. He looks like he's sixty, not in his nineties.

"Grandfather, I want you to meet my girlfriend, Mackenzie Harper, otherwise known as Mack."

His grandfather moves slowly forward to greet me. "Well now, you are mighty pretty," he says, taking my hand.

I swallow around the lump of emotion that threatens to choke me and settle when Dean places his hand on my back as I look at his grandfather. "Thank you."

"Can we keep her?" Jacob asks his grandson.

"I'm working on that, grandfather."

Jacob sits down and pulls me down beside him.

"So, tell me...what brought tears to your eyes when you saw me?"

I look at Dean, wondering where to begin. "I'm going to find Grandmother while you two chat." Dean quickly kisses me on the forehead as he leaves the room.

"Now I'm even more curious than before." Jacob gives me a quizzical look.

"May I call you, Jacob?" I ask.

He smiles and pats my hand. "Seeing as you're practically family, that would be fine. Although, I hope you will call me grandfather, eventually."

"I might." I take a deep breath and start my story, or rather theirs, "If I told you that Dean and I met in Cape Elizabeth at Degan House, what would that mean to you?" I watch him carefully and see the color drain from his face slightly, his hands begin to tremble. "Jacob, I found a diary dated 1947, written by a Rose Degan. She was in love with you, wasn't she?"

Jacob nods. "Yes," he whispers, looking away from me and appears to be lost in his own thoughts.

"She never married Richard," I announce.

He turns back toward me, his eyes fill with some unknown emotion. "Pardon?"

"This isn't easy, Jacob, but Rose was running away

to be with you, when she," I take a deep breath, "she lost her footing and fell over the cliffs. Jacob, she did love you so very much, she didn't leave you for Richard like her father told you. She didn't get the chance to leave with you."

Jacob looks toward the windows and the garden beyond before he looks back at me. He's clearly agitated, and it breaks her heart that she's the cause of it. "I don't know what to say."

"Jacob, why did you wait a few days to call Degan House to speak to Rose? Why not look for her that night? You knew she was pregnant? I have so many questions. None of it makes sense to me."

"I don't remember," he says abruptly, cutting me off.

I'm a bit surprised at Jacob's response.

Dean comes back into the room, looking first at me, who is upset, then his grandfather. "Is everyone okay?" he asks as he approaches Mack, wiping her tears away.

"I think so," I reply.

"Sorry for cutting this short, but Grandmother is waiting in the parlor and was about to head this way as she's getting rather impatient. I've been sent to get you both." He grins. "She's keen to meet you, Mack."

He's leading me out of the room, followed by his grandfather, when I notice a photograph sitting in a lovely frame on the bookcase. I walk over to have a closer look. "Who's that?" I ask, pointing at the woman in the photograph. I've seen the photograph before and know who it is, but Jacob having it on his bookshelf, when he married someone else, doesn't make any sense.

Jacob replies, "Eliza, my wife."

"Mack, what is it?" Dean asks.

"The woman in this picture. It's Rose!" I exclaim.

"Mack, that's my grandmother," Dean says, his voice laced with confusion.

I hear Dean, but I can't think properly because all the blood seems to be running through my head and ears.

It can't be? Can it?

"This is the same picture Thomas has that Rose left for him. That's Rose, not Eliza," I whisper.

"What? Mack, that's impossible." Dean searches my face, realizing I'm serious.

He looks toward his grandfather, and then his grandmother as she walks in. I take one look at her before I lose all color and drop like a ton of bricks in a dead faint.

Dean manages to catch her...*just.*

"MACK, COME ON. PLEASE WAKE UP." DEAN SITS ON the sofa in his grandfather's study with me cradled in his arms. "Why does Mack think the picture is of Rose?" he asks his grandparents.

"Dean, what are you talking about?" his grandmother asks.

"The photograph of the two of you taken before you got married, when you were pregnant with my father. Why does Mack think it's Rose?"

"Because she is Rose. Rose Elizabeth Degan, Eliza," I answer Dean's question. "Am I right?" I mumble.

"There were only two pictures taken, we have one ..." Eliza says quietly, her voice trailing off.

"You gave the other one to Thomas, which is how I saw it."

Sitting down, Eliza looks at me. "How do you know this?"

"You're Rose?" Dean says.

His grandmother slowly nods her head as he admits, "Mack found the diary that you wrote when you met my grandfather. Also, Thomas and Richard helped fill in the blanks."

"Thomas?" Eliza whispers.

"Your brother," I tell Eliza, frowning.

"No…no…no…you're wrong. Thomas died in 1953 in Korea…didn't he?" Eliza asks, barely able to finish as the color drains from her cheeks, so Jacob sits next to her and wraps an arm around her trembling shoulders.

I ask them the one question that I need to know the answer to. "Why? Why pretend you were dead? And what do we call you now?"

"I've been Eliza longer than I was Rose. Please use Eliza… Can you tell us about Thomas? Then we'll tell you, our story."

I cling to Dean. "Thomas is the owner of Rose Cottage, which I rented for the summer. It used to be known as Degan House. I found your diary and started reading it. All this time, Thomas had no idea about the photograph or the message you had written to him. After he thought you died, he couldn't bring himself to read the comic until I read about it in the diary. It was only then that he found the photograph and message."

"But he's dead. How? I don't understand," Eliza says.

"Why do you think he's dead?" I question anxiously, trying to make sense of everything.

"Mack, I took Eliza back to see Thomas in 1954. She missed him terribly, only to be told by her father he'd been killed six months earlier in Korea," Jacob answers.

I'm not sure I hear correctly. "Your parents knew?" I gasp.

"Yes, or rather, my father did," Eliza whispers with tears in her eyes, "Please tell me about Thomas," she begs softly.

"He did serve in Korea, but he didn't die. In fact, he has become a good friend to Dean and me. He loves to fish and taught my six-year-old nephew. I would say he still gets up to trouble with Levi, who we've met briefly."

"All this time wasted," Eliza cries.

"Will you tell us your story now?"

Eliza wipes her eyes. "I will." She composes herself and clasps one of Jacob's hands with hers on her lap. "You already know about everything up to that night, yes?"

"Yes," I reply.

Eliza still looks beautiful at eighty-nine. She wears her silver hair pulled back into a bun and it emphasizes her high cheekbones, small button nose, and her skin looks to have aged well. She wears a deep purple dress on her slim figure with low-heeled black and purple ballerina pumps. Very stylish, and both Rose and Jacob still look so much in love, after all these years together. It make sense now as to why Jacob was so in love with Eliza.

Dean pulls me closer into his arms and sits back further into the cushions. "We might as well get comfortable. Are you okay, Mack?" he asks, kissing me briefly, but tenderly.

"Yes. Are you?"

"Everything always is with you in my arms."

"Good answer," I whisper, snuggling into him. He always makes me feel loved and cherished with his concern for my wellbeing.

Eliza sighs. "I was on my way to meet Jacob. I'd taken the path along the cliffs when Richard came running up to me. He begged me not to go and kept grabbing me, begging me to stay and marry him. I told him about the baby, thinking he would let me go then, but no such luck. I started getting worried because I didn't want Jacob to think I'd changed my mind if I wasn't there by eleven."

Eliza can't continue so Jacob carries on from where she left off. "I knew Rose was going to take the cliff path to meet me. I walked along it from town to meet her, and that's when I heard her arguing with Richard. I went running up and pried his fingers off Rose. I took her into my arms before putting her behind me. Richard made a grab for her again and ended up knocking Rose's bag over the cliff edge into the ocean."

"So that's how the clothes washed ashore," Dean states.

Eliza nods her head.

"Yes. After that, he seemed to calm down and I begged him to tell everyone Rose had gone over the cliffs. He refused at first, but Rose knew something about him, so he agreed in return for her silence," Jacob says.

I'm too stunned to speak, but Dean isn't. "So, you faked your own death?"

"It wasn't planned that way. Rose really was going to run away with me to be my wife, but pretending she'd died seemed the safest option. That night, I met her parents for the first time and her father made it more than clear that he didn't want us anywhere near each other. Her father had many influential friends and was a tough man. He would have come after us with everything he had, and all we wanted was to be left alone to get on with our lives, together."

"But what about the phone call to Degan House days later. Thomas heard your father telling your mother about Jacob calling and telling him you had married Richard. You said your father knew you were alive?" I ask, needing answers.

"We left that night to go to Boston and stayed with Eleanor, Jacob's sister. After about a week of living there, Jacob arranged for us to be married. We knew I was really pregnant by then, and he didn't want me showing without having the paper to prove we were actually married. He also wanted assurance that if my father discovered the truth, it would be harder for him to take me away from him as I would be Jacob's wife." Eliza pauses. "After a few days, Jacob thought perhaps he should ring to ask to speak to me and see what my father or mother had to say. I didn't like the idea but went along with it. My father was awful to Jacob and told him that I had married Richard and miscarried his child. I cried for the rest of the day."

Jacob wipes the tears from Eliza's eyes. "Then it

was maybe three weeks later that I opened the door, and my father was standing there. Jacob was at work, and I didn't know what to do so I stepped outside with him. My father was so angry and said I really was dead to him, and I better not let my mother know I was alive and obviously in good health. I asked my father how he knew, and he told me Richard had told him that I was with child when I died. However, it was only the week before that he'd discovered I was actually alive. Apparently, a friend of his had seen me in Boston and asked my father about me. My father then went to see Richard again, and got the full story out of him."

We sit on the sofa in silence. You could hear a pin drop. I feel overwhelmed with the turn of events. Rose is alive. I knew there was something *off* with the information we've uncovered. Although I hoped for a happy ending for Rose, I certainly hadn't expected one. "So, you eventually went back to see Thomas?" I ask, finding my voice.

"Yes. It was 1954. Rose had missed Thomas so much. Her mother had died in 1951 so there was no fear of her finding out about Rose. We had a car by then, so we drove up to Cape Elizabeth. Her father was home. We asked him about Thomas, and he told us that he had died in Korea. It broke Rose's heart and she cried for weeks. I can't believe that bastard lied to us. I guess we should have expected it, but we didn't, not about something like that," Jacob replies.

"We have to see Thomas." Eliza wipes her eyes.

"Grandmother, I think this is going to be one heck of a shock for him. Let Mack and me break it to him and then we'll arrange a get together or something. But we need to go easy. Up until Mack read your diary, he actually thought you'd died hating him."

Eliza brings her hand up to her mouth. "I loved him... He has always been in my heart."

"He has always loved you, Eliza. He told me that himself." I wonder. "What did you know about Richard?"

Eliza and Jacob exchange a look. "He loved Rose a lot, we really believed that, but Rose had discovered that he preferred...men," Jacob says.

"Oh." I wasn't expecting that at all, but all of a sudden, I remember about Rose's friend, Jayne. "What about Jayne? Did she know you were still alive?"

Eliza smiles. "I got in touch with Jayne about two weeks after we left Cape Elizabeth, and I knew for once, she would keep my secret because she has, all these years. Jayne was, and still is, my dearest friend.

She's gone away with her husband now. It was her house we went to the day of your mother's garden party. Would you believe that she actually married Jacob's best friend from the engineering company that he started to work at all those years ago."

"Thank you for telling us your story. I can't tell you how much it means to me, knowing you're alive and lived all these years, happily married to Jacob. It broke my heart when I thought you'd died, and that Jacob had been told you'd left him for another man," I say, close to tears again.

Dean stands and moves over to the desk to retrieve a box of tissues, offering some to me and his grandmother. He kneels in front of me and pulls me close so he can wipe my tears away, then kisses me. "Come here." He takes me into his arms for a much-needed hug.

"Dean, may I have a word with you, please?" his grandmother asks. She starts to leave via a door on the opposite side from where everyone entered.

"Will you be, okay?" he questions.

"Dean, go. I'll be fine." I smile to reassure him.

He still looks apprehensive. "I won't be long."

"Don't worry about me."

I sit quietly with Jacob as Dean and his grandmother disappeared through the other door. Jacob looks at me and smiles slightly.

"So, what did Eliza write?" He roars with laughter when he sees the look on my face. "That good, huh? Might give me a heart attack now."

I giggle. "It's pretty hot stuff, I can assure you."

"Mmm, hot stuff. That's what she was back then, she still is. She's the only woman I've ever loved. I can still remember the first day I saw her. I thought I was dreaming. It was a rescue at sea, and I was helping out on land. Heading back to get a warm drink, I happened to look up and glance into the crowd, and there she was." Lost in his thoughts. "She was the most beautiful woman I'd ever seen, and I felt my heart somersault in my chest. It was love at first sight for me, and before I knew it, my legs were carrying me over to where she was standing."

Jacob wipes his eyes, setting me off again with the waterworks. "We introduced ourselves and I didn't want to ever leave her. I wanted to carry her away with me and keep her forever."

"Which you did, but a month later." I smile.

"Yes, I did. The only thing I regret about what happened back then is that we didn't go and get married before going to see her father. We should have done that and told him instead of pretending that she died. He probably would have acted the same, but at least there might have been a chance of Thomas being in our lives as he got older."

Eliza comes back into the room. "Jacob, what have you been saying to upset Dean's girl again?" she scolds, but there is affection in her tone.

I smile. "He was telling me how it was love at first sight when he saw you. A bit like Dean and me, really."

Eliza sits down next to her husband. Dean moves to sit down next to me and takes my hand in his, lacing our fingers together. "Like us, Mack."

"If you want the truth, Mack, neither his grandmother nor I thought we would see the day when he would fall in love so not only have you made us happy telling us about Thomas, but you have made us ecstatic by loving our grandson. So, thank you."

I smile at both of Dean's grandparents. "I want you to know I love Dean so much. He has become part of me in such a short time." I turn to Dean and place a tender kiss on his lips.

"Now you've made me cry," Eliza says, wiping at her eyes again.

Dean stands, pulling me up from the sofa. "We're

going to go and rest for a while before heading out.
We'll see you before we leave."

"Make sure you do," Eliza says.

I hug Eliza and Jacob.

"You take good care of her, you hear?" Jacob gives
him a stern look.

Dean looks at me. "Yes, sir," he replies, looking at
his grandfather.

Chapter 28

WE walk out of the study and Dean escorts me through to the back stairs and up to his room so that Martha won't see us and engage in conversation. All we want is to be alone.

I'm still shocked after discovering Rose is still alive, having been living all these years as Eliza.

"Mack, come and lie down. You look drained."

I move over to Dean and wrap my arms around his waist. "Don't let go."

He picks me up in his arms and carries me to his bed. "I don't intend to."

He lays down on the bed with me cradled in his arms. "I love you, Dean," I whisper before falling asleep.

As I start to wake, I forgot where I am and why, but I certainly recognize the body holding me.

I smile, feeling full of joy, knowing that Rose hasn't died and has lived a long life. Seventy years with the love of her life, Jacob. I don't know how to break the news to Thomas, but hopefully, he won't be that upset, now that he has his beloved sister back and her husband. He's gained a large family as well from what Dean has already told me about his relations.

I wrap my arms around a sleeping Dean and kiss his chest. "I'm so thankful that you took the trip to meet me in Cape Elizabeth the day that I spoke with Martha, rather than ignoring the call," I whisper.

"So am I."

I lift my head and meet Dean's eyes. "I didn't know you were awake."

"Been lying here awhile, thinking about everything that's happened today, and since I met you. I wouldn't change any of it." He gently squeezes me.

He slides slightly down so his face is level with mine, then smooths my hair back from my eyes. He uses his finger to trace my eyebrows, down my lightly freckled nose, and to my lips before he caresses them. I open my mouth slightly.

"Marry me, Mack," he blurts.

I freeze.

"I didn't mean to blurt it out like that," he admits, sheepishly, before he continues, "I love you. Right from the first day, Mack. I don't want to lose you." He sees the tears swimming in my eyes. "I know we haven't known each other long. We can even have a long engagement. I just want to know you're mine."

I give a tear-filled laugh. "Yes."

He smiles and gently caresses my face as I watch the nerves from a few minutes ago starts to dwindle, and are replaced with a deep yearning.

Reaching into his pocket, he produces a very special ring, and taking hold of my left hand, he slides it slowly down my finger while he holds my gaze. "My grandmother took me out of the room to give me this ring. She said it was the ring my grandfather gave her seventy years ago. It had belonged to my great-grandmother."

He takes a minute to get his emotions in check before he continues, "She took it off her finger, Mack, to give it to me. She said it had never once left her finger, and that she wanted me to give it to you because she saw the love we have for each other. She also thought it was fitting for the woman who returned her brother to her to wear it." He leans in and kisses my lips ever so gently.

I have no idea what to say. I'm touched beyond words that Eliza gave her engagement ring to Dean for me. No wonder Dean had been all choked up telling me what his grandmother said.

"Let me look." He raises my hand so we both can admire his grandmother's ring. The square cut diamond is set in platinum and surrounded with small sapphires. He kisses my finger. "It looks amazing, and it's a perfect fit."

"Yes, it does, and I think it's a good omen that it fits perfectly. Hopefully, we'll have seventy plus years together as well."

"I hope so. I think we need to celebrate."

I feel much better as I move from the bed and stand to the side. I smile at a surprised Dean. I start to unfasten my blouse and place it on the chair to the side, and then I remove my skirt, all the time holding Dean's gaze.

I give him my back and slide my panties down my legs, kicking them toward the chair, followed by my bra. I can hear Dean's breathing change, as the bed moves slightly, I turn toward him, only to discover Dean yanking his clothes off, and letting them fly any which way.

I laugh and give him a wicked grin. "Mmm, you look good enough to eat."

He groans with laughter. "You're going to kill me, Mack."

"Oh, I don't think so," I reply, and crawling across the bed on my hands and knees toward a very aroused Dean.

Chapter 29

In the morning, I'm sitting on Dean's lap in the kitchen of Rose Cottage and sharing a pot of steaming coffee, while we make a list of what we need to organize for our wedding. I'm not quite sure how I ended up announcing this weekend was fine for a wedding. *A moment of insanity?*

Yesterday had been an amazing day, full of highs. Not only had I discovered Rose and Jacob had been together all these years, but I was now wearing Eliza's engagement ring as my very own, which raises the question, "Dean? Do you think your mother would like to come looking at wedding dresses with my mother and I?" I see the shock on Dean's face. "She's going to be my mother-in-law so the least I can do is try and get along with her. But if she's rude again, all bets are off."

"Tell me when and where and I'll let my mother know." He smiles.

"Thomas is here," I blurt, spotting him through the window.

"Mack, he'll probably be shocked at first, but he has a family now. He's no longer alone. He's stronger than you think."

"Am I interrupting something?" Thomas asks, coming into the kitchen.

I stand, laughing, and then walk over to Thomas. "We got engaged yesterday, Thomas. We want to be married here, at Rose Cottage, this weekend."

"Oh, my." He clears his throat. "Congratulations to you both." Thomas hugs me, and then shakes Dean's hand.

"Sit down, Thomas. That's not all our news," I say, my voice tight with nerves.

He sits down and glances from me to Dean. "Well, you can't be pregnant yet. Can you?"

"No, I'm not pregnant, Thomas. This is my engagement ring." I lift my hand up so Thomas can see the ring.

"That's lovely, Mack." Then he turns to Dean. "Is it a family heirloom?"

"Yes, it is," Dean answers.

"Thomas, there's no easy way to say this." I take a deep breath. "Yesterday, when we went to visit Dean's grandparents, we discovered that Eliza, Jacob's wife and Dean's grandmother, is actually Rose, your sister." Thomas's eyes focus completely on me. "Rose didn't die that night, Thomas. Rose and Jacob blackmailed Richard into telling your parents that he saw her go over the cliffs."

Dean passes Thomas and me a glass of water and continues the story, "Rose came back to see you and tell you the truth in 1954, only to be told by your father that you'd died in Korea. All these years, Thomas, she thought that you were dead."

Thomas leans forward in his chair and drops his face into his hands. I go over to him and wrap an arm around his shoulders. I feel him shaking while his tears fall silently.

He lifts his head. "After all these years. Because of the both of you." He shakes his head. "I can't take it all in. I never expected any of this." He looks at me then Dean. "You're my great-nephew?"

I wipe at my eyes. "Eliza and Jacob will be here this weekend for our wedding. She's waiting for your call, Thomas."

"I can talk to her, after all these years. What's she like?" he asks softly with excitement.

"She looks about twenty years younger than she is. In fact, Jacob certainly doesn't look his age, either. Thomas, she was as shaken as you are when she learned you were alive. She said she has missed you so much over the years. She still wishes to go by Eliza, though."

"I can understand that. After all, that's what she's used for a very long time... So, she gave you her engagement ring," Thomas says, looking at Dean.

"She did. She said she wanted the woman of my heart, who returned her brother to her to have her ring."

"Then I guess if you want a wedding here this weekend, you better get a move on." Thomas laughs.

I've relieved Thomas is taking the news about Eliza so well. In a way, it's a dream come true for me because not only have I fallen in love with Dean, but Thomas as well. After I marry Dean, we will all be a family. I also know one little lad who will be thrilled to bits to discover Thomas is going to be part of the family.

He stands "I'll take her number, if you will, then leave you to it."

I hand him the number that I've already written down for him. "Here you go. Are you okay?"

He pulls me into his arms and holds me close. "I'm more than okay. Thank you so much. You're the daughter I never had," he whispers, close to tears.

THOMAS SAT IN HIS LIVING ROOM WITH SILENT TEARS running down his face as he stared at the piece of paper with his sister's telephone number written on. Never in a million years did he ever think that she was alive and living her life with the man she'd fallen in love with so many years before.

He'd always had a love-hate relationship with his father but hearing the lies their father had told Rose made him angry. So many years lost. So many years of being alone without any family around him when all along he still had his sister, her husband, and their offspring. His heart ached for all that he'd missed, and as he thought about Rose, now Eliza, a soft smile crossed his lips.

Sighing heavily, he grabbed a handful of tissues and cleaned himself up before he reached for the telephone that sat on the table beside his chair—better to not waste any more time.

His hands shook as he carefully dialed the number, and he waited...and then, when his call was answered, he heard his sister's voice as his own failed him.

"Hello, is anyone there," she whispered before Thomas heard her gasp. "Thomas, is that you?"

"Yes," he replied in a strangled voice.

"Thomas," Eliza whispered, softly crying. "I can't believe that I have you back... So many years... Oh, Thomas, how I wish . . ." His sister broke down into sobs, and hearing her, Thomas cried with her.

Their call stayed connected and eventually, Thomas pulled himself together enough to start thinking again.

"Rose... I mean Eliza, will you tell me about you and Jacob? About your life? I need to hear you talk to me."

He heard his sister sniffling before she admitted,

"Leaving you was the most difficult, Thomas. That's why I left you that photograph in your comic. I always wondered why you never tried to contact me."

"That was all my fault for never opening the comic until Mack told me that you'd written about it in your diary...So many years Rose."

He could hear the smile in her voice and the affection that she had for Jacob as she continued, "After that night, we lived with Jacob's sister in Boston until we'd saved enough for a house of our own. Jacob had a really good job and quickly moved up in the engineering company. Over the years we invested in the company and by the time Jacob retired he was nearly running it." She paused, and chuckled. "Do you remember Jayne?"

Thomas had to think because it was a long time ago that she wanted him to remember, and then the memory of her best friend popped into his head, and he laughed. "She always wore make-up and Father would complain behind her back about the kind of men she'd meet dressed up like she was."

"Yes! That's right. Well, Jayne is still my best friend today and she married a colleague of Jacob's a few years after I left." She sighed. "I so wish we hadn't lost all those years."

Smiling through his tears, Thomas said, "We have now, Rose. We have now."

He sat back with a grin splitting his face, enjoying hearing her voice as he got to know more about his Rose's life.

Chapter 30

IT'S THREE HOURS BEFORE THE WEDDING, AND regardless of how many people have told me that it's bad luck to see the groom before the wedding, I insist I am going to be there to see Thomas and Eliza meet for the first time in seventy years.

I haven't dressed in my wedding finery yet, so I head downstairs in search of Dean, so I can watch the reunion with him.

When we told Thomas that Rose has been happily married to Jacob for all these years, it was harder than we both thought it would be, even Dean is all choked up.

Brother and sister have talked on the phone daily

since the news has broken, and there has been a lot of tears, as well as laughter.

As I enter the kitchen, I find a very nervous Thomas and a very hot-looking Dean sitting at the table, trying to wait patiently for Eliza and Jacob, who are being driven to the cottage by Dean's parents.

"Hey, beautiful. What are you doing down here in jeans? There's a wedding happening in a few hours."

I walk over to Dean and wrap my arms around him from behind. "I have it on good authority that the gorgeous bride has it all under control."

I kiss Dean on the top of his head and walk around the table to Thomas to give him a hug as well.

"What if she doesn't like me?" Thomas asks in a worried voice.

"Oh, Thomas, Eliza said you have always been in her heart. You could have two heads, and she would still love you. Please don't worry. In fact, I bet Eliza is probably thinking the same as you. Seventy years is a long time."

I walk back to Dean and sit on his lap, feeling awfully nervous for the reunion.

Thomas pulls himself together, sits up straight in his chair, and reaches inside his jacket to take out an envelope. "This here is your wedding present." He taps it on the tabletop. "I want you both to know that up until last week, I didn't have any family. Now I have a large one, and it includes you both. I certainly don't have anyone to pass anything on to, although Lucas has spoken up for the *Our Gang* comics," he says with a wistful smile touching his lips before he continues, "Having said all that, because of you both, I have my sister back, and that's worth more than what's in here."

Thomas holds the envelope out to me, but my hands shake far too much to open it so I pass it to Dean. He opens it and can't believe what he's looking at.

"Dean, what is it?" I ask.

He has to swallow around the lump in his throat. "It's the deed to Rose Cottage, in both of our names."

We look at Thomas. "You're both at home here at Rose Cottage, and I'm getting too old to look after it. I want you both to have it, and to live here and raise a family. Besides, I happen to know the local school needs a teacher, and I have it on good authority that Auntie Mack is a very good one, although a bit bossy."

I laugh in delight, grinning through my tears. I certainly hadn't expected the cottage as a wedding present, but I should have known Thomas would do something like this. Rose Cottage is where it all started—not just for myself and Dean, but for Rose and Jacob all those years ago.

Standing, I meet Thomas, who is walking toward us for a very big hug. "I don't know what to say, Thomas," I admit, more tears running down my face.

"A thank you will suffice." He chuckles.

I pull back and take hold of Dean's hand. "Thank you. I do love it here." I look at Dean. "If it's okay with Dean then we'll live here. Besides, someone has to make sure you don't get into any trouble."

Thomas chuckles. "Just make sure those babies appear sooner rather than later. I'm not a spring chicken anymore."

"I'm sure if Dean has his way, we'll get started on that pretty soon." I blush.

"With plenty of practice, I'm sure we'll get it right." Dean chuckles.

We hear a car pull up outside, which stops the laughter, and panic flickers across Thomas's face.

I take Thomas's hand. "Come on, Thomas, you can do this. Just remember Eliza and Jacob are going to be as nervous as you are."

Dean opens the back door and holds it open as Thomas steps out, holding my hand really tight as though he expects me to bolt. Dean follows us outside and runs over to open the car door for his grandparents.

His grandfather steps out first, and then turns back toward the car to help Eliza out. With Dean on one side of his grandmother, and Jacob on the other, they make their way toward us.

I can feel Thomas shaking, and from the look of things, so are Eliza and Jacob. Meeting Dean's eyes, I nudge Thomas forward at the same time Eliza lets go of both Dean and Jacob to wrap her arms around Thomas. They are both sobbing as though their hearts will burst.

I take two steps straight into Dean's arms and cry all over him. He runs his hands up and down my back in a soothing motion.

I finally manage to get myself under control and wipe my face on the handkerchief Dean's father passes me. "Thank you."

Eliza takes ahold of Jacob's hand and pulls him slightly forward to meet her brother. She had written in her diary how much she'd wished that Thomas and Jacob could get to know each other. Although it was a long time ago when she had expressed that wish, it was now coming true.

Eliza turns toward me and moves closer. I let go of Dean and walk straight into Eliza's embrace. "Thank you, Mack. You have no idea how much everything you have done means to Jacob and me," she whispers.

I pull away and wipe my eyes giving both Thomas and Jacob a hug before I return to Dean's waiting arms.

I TURN AROUND TO TAKE THE FIRST LOOK IN THE FULL-length mirror.

I don't think I'm unattractive but I have never been one to pay a lot of attention to preening. After all, I'm a schoolteacher of small children and classes tend to be messy. But when I turn and see myself in the mirror, I'm stunned. Staring back at me is . . . "A princess," Melinda says, as she enters the room.

"Is this really me?" I whisper.

"You are so beautiful. Today, you are simply radiant. Are you really happy, Mack?" Melinda asks, taking hold of my hand.

"Sis, I've never been as happy. I love Dean so much and I can't imagine my life without him." I pause. "I also can't imagine living anywhere other than here."

"What are you trying to tell me?"

I smile. "Thomas has given Rose Cottage to Dean and me, as a wedding present. Apparently, Lucas has claimed all the *Our Gang* comics, and he doesn't have anyone else to leave this to. He said that we're his family, and he wants us to have it and raise a family here."

"So, you're going to move here?" Melinda questions.

I nod.

"This is what you've always wanted, Mack. A house out of the city near the beach with a good loving man and lots of kids. A huge part of your dream has come true, and I'm really happy for you," Melinda says.

"Thank you."

"You do realize that Lucas will always want to come and stay with you?"

"As long as there's no school, he's always welcome. You all are." I grin.

We turn upon hearing the door open. "What are

you girls doing in here? You're supposed to be downstairs."

"Mom," Melinda winks at me, and then turns back to our mother, "I was giving Mack the birds and the bees talk."

Our mother walks further into the room, walking around Mack with tears coming to her eyes. "You look stunning... Your father is going to cry like a baby." She then turns her attention to Melinda. "And I'm sure she doesn't need the bird and the bees talk considering the very handsome groom downstairs," she comments, fanning herself.

"Mom, you're not supposed to notice things like that," Melinda says in fake shock.

"I have eyes."

"Mom..." we moan in unison.

"Come on, there's a nervous man downstairs wanting to make you his wife, and your very nervous father is waiting to give you away."

I take another look at myself in the mirror and allow my mom and Melinda to escort me out of the room and downstairs to my father.

DEAN WAS STANDING IN THE GAZEBO WHILE HE WAITED for Mack to appear. His nerves danced as the minutes ticked by while he wondered where his bride was. There wasn't a huge amount of family present, but only meeting Mack's parents, with her father giving him the third degree, hadn't helped his nerves much. All he wanted was his Mack.

Thomas was sitting close by, waiting to act as best man. He was still a bit shaky after his meeting with Rose—a very emotional time.

It took Mack about half an hour to calm down. Then she was mortified to realize both her eyes were puffy, so after cutting chunks of cucumber, had disappeared back upstairs saying she would see them all at the wedding.

Thomas came to stand beside him. "You're one lucky man."

"Don't I know . . ." Dean trailed off when he caught sight of Mack in her long, fitted, white, strapless dress covered in lace. She started walking toward him and he couldn't take his eyes from her. She truly was the most beautiful woman he had ever seen, but most importantly, beautiful on the inside, too. He swallowed around the lump in his throat and tried to take hold of his emotions. As he did so, Dean glanced at his grandmother and noticed her crying softly into his grandfather's arms.

He looked back at Mack and spotted his mother with her handkerchief guarding her eyes as well. She had apologized to Mack for being so rude and had welcomed her into the family. Mack had accepted the olive branch, and even asked her to accompany herself, along with her mother, when she went looking for a wedding dress.

Lucas came to a stop at Dean's side with a huge grin on his face. Dressed in a pale grey suit, dark grey shirt, and silver tie, he looked so handsome. He leaned toward Dean. "Don't forget, when you're my uncle, you have to buy me a present and my birthday's next week. And seeing as you don't know how to play, maybe you can ask my grandma how to play strip poker. She says it's very easy and stimulatering, or something like that."

Dean laughed and turned back to Mack, who was about to reach his side. He was thankful she'd decided to rent Rose Cottage for the summer. Grateful that she'd discovered his grandmother's diary, which had brought him to the Cottage, and eventually brought his grandmother back together with her brother, after all those years apart. They'd come full circle, and he couldn't be happier.

Mack passed her flowers to Melinda and turned to look at Dean. When their eyes met, they realized this was where they belonged, with each other...at Rose Cottage.

Epilogue

TWELVE MONTHS LATER

I SIT WITH MY FEET UP AND MY BACK RESTING AGAINST my husband with a soft smile on my lips as I watch Thomas, Eliza, and Jacob interact across the room. My belly is hugely swollen with a nine-month-old baby bump, my ankles are pretty swollen too. Dean fusses over me constantly and a few times I've had to bite my tongue so I won't snap at him. I know he means well, and really, I'm only frustrated that I can't do everything I could a few months before.

Dean loves to caress my stomach and each night he reads a Beatrix Potter story to our child so that he or she will recognize his voice. We are impatient to meet our child and can't wait for the arrival, which will hopefully be sooner rather than later.

Hearing the raucous laughter coming from his grandfather, Dean laughs and nuzzles into my neck. "I can't believe we have all this," he whispers, sending shivers down my spine. "And all because of you, my beautiful wife." He kisses my shoulder, his large hands caressing my belly.

"I've never been so happy." My hands cover his.

"You're my happiness—" He stills. "What was that?" he questions, straightening behind me. "Your stomach went hard."

I can't answer because the most incredible pain rips through me while I hold on to Dean's hand for dear life. When the pain subsides, I gasp for breath, sweat appearing on my forehead and panic clear in my eyes.

Dean quickly settles me back on the sofa as he moves in the front of me...only just missing being caught in the release of my water breaking. "Oh, Dean."

He laughs and I throw him a scathing look, but luckily for him, his grandma Eliza interrupts with her hand on his back. "Is it time, honey?"

"Her water broke." He pales. "Oh!" Until he said the words out loud, I don't think it properly registered with him just what was happening.

"You've got this, Dean. Let me get the men out of the room and I'll call for an ambulance." Eliza moves quickly for her age and ushers Jacob and Thomas out of the room without allowing them to catch a glimpse of me. I'd be laughing if another contraction isn't creeping up on me.

I grab ahold of Dean's hand, squeezing with all my might as I try to concentrate on the breathing and panting sequences that I've been taught to do in the birthing class, however I squeeze my eyes closed and can't help hold my breath as the intense pain takes hold.

Dean leans forward to wipe my eyes as tears leak from between by lashes. "I love you," he whispers.

"I'm scared," I admit, my voice breaking. "I'm also uncomfortable in wet panties."

Before I can speak another pain take my breath away. I must be close, the contractions are so close together that I feel panic starting to set in. Dean crouches in front of me and grasps my hands. "I have you, honey."

As the pain subsides, I turn tear filled eyes up to his. "Tell me what to do for you," he begs.

My lips quiver. "Remove my panties...*please*."

He smiles and catches my lips twitch with amusement. "One of my favorite jobs... Can you stand?"

"If you help me."

Dean slips his arm around my waist and hauls me to my feet when I say, "Be quick before another hits."

He moves me away from the puddle on the floor and slips his hands beneath my dress. He grabs my panties and quickly tugs them down my legs, helping me to step out of them. "I have an idea," he comments.

Quickly moving to the sofa, he yanks the throw off and folds it in half before he places it on the seat. He takes hold of my hand and guides me to a dry chair. "I'm going to lift the back of your dress, so you're not sitting on the wet part."

Once I'm seated, I'm panting my way through another contraction and when the sudden urge to push hits, my eyes snap wide.

It's too soon. I can't be ready to push. Not yet. "Will you look?"

"Look?" Dean queries, his eyes widening in panic when he registers what I mean. "As in *look?*" He pointedly stares below my belly. "Okay." He kneels at my feet. "What am I looking for?"

"I got the urge to push with the last contraction. See if you can see something...anything," I urge.

Gripping my dress, he moves it over my stomach and ducking down he spreads my legs. "I have no idea what I'm supposed to be looking for."

"Spread me open and see if you can see a baby's head or something. I don't know. I just know you're supposed to check me."

He waits until another pain subsides and then he gently spreads me, and stills . . .

"Uncle Dean, are you stroking Auntie Mack's p—"

"Lucas Cartwright do not finish that sentence," his mother screeches, barging into the room. "Go wait with your father."

"Um…" Melinda comes to a sudden stop behind the sofa, "…what…"

"She needs to push," Dean answers her befuddled silence.

"Oh!" Melinda says in panic and dashes around to Mack's side. "Pant, honey. Don't push yet, just pant through it and the paramedics should be here soon."

"They're here." The emergency lights flash through the window.

Moments later they come barging into the room.

～

Dᴇᴀɴ ʜᴀs ᴛᴇᴀʀs sᴛʀᴇᴀᴍɪɴɢ ᴅᴏᴡɴ ʜɪs ꜰᴀᴄᴇ ᴛʜᴀᴛ mingle with mine while we cuddle our just born daughter, *Rose Elizabeth Evans.*

The hospital staff have checked our daughter out before laying her on my chest while they cleaned me up.

Rose Elizabeth has been impatient to arrive and had been born within thirteen minutes of them arriving at the hospital.

Our daughter has a head full of black hair, and as I manage to get her latched onto a breast so that she can feed, Dean strokes his daughter's soft head. He buries his face into my neck where he places a tender kiss. "Thank you," he whispers, overcome with emotion.

I reach up and curl my arm to the back of Dean's head. I hold him against me while I wish that I was already in the private room so that Dean could climb into bed with us.

Tʜɪɴɢs ʜᴀᴅ ɢᴏᴛᴛᴇɴ ᴀ ʙɪᴛ sʜᴀᴋʏ ᴛᴏᴡᴀʀᴅ ᴛʜᴇ ᴇɴᴅ and Dean had gone lightheaded. It had only been pure determination not to let Mack down that had kept him on his feet.

But damn, he was a Daddy and that thought filled him with excitement. The precious little bundle, nuzzling at Mack's breast was a miracle—a miracle that they'd made together.

"Mack," the nurse interrupted, "do you want to have a shower before we move you up to your room for the night?" Dean had forgotten others were in the room with them.

"I'll probably feel better if I do." Mack released the hold she had on Dean, and with reluctance, slipped her nipple from her daughter's mouth. Rose had fallen asleep as she'd nuzzled her.

She smiled when Dean helped cover her breast, but the look of panic on his face when she passed Rose into his arms made her chuckle. "You have this."

Dean didn't even acknowledge her as he looked at the small bundle in his arms. His first time holding his daughter, and the emotion on his face had more tears welling in Mack's eyes. That first image of Father and Daughter would stay with her forever.

~

I LAY BACK ON THE BED WITH DEAN CUDDLING ME from behind while we watch Eliza cuddle her great granddaughter. Jacob sits beside her, his eyes watering as he strokes one of Rose's small hands.

Dean kisses me on the side of my face. "So precious," he whispers into my ear. "You've given me so much, Mack. You'll never know how grateful I am."

I softly shake my head. "I wouldn't have the most beautiful baby if it wasn't for you. I wouldn't be as happy as I've been since I've met you. You're everything to me, Dean. Everything." I turn my face and bury it in Dean's chest as his hands threaded through my long hair.

"Eww, you're always kissing." Lucas bursts into the room with a look of disgust on his face.

I take one look at our seven-year-old nephew and chuckle.

"Just wait until you've grown up into a young man, then you won't be saying, 'Eww,'" Dean comments.

Lucas became lost in his baby cousin the second his eyes landed on him. He slowly moves over and wiggles his bottom onto the chair beside Eliza. He reaches out and strokes Rose's head. "I think I like my new cousin, even if it is a *girl*." Lucas is too engrossed in our daughter to notice the amusement on the faces of everyone in the room.

Eliza is the first to break the spell. "Who brought you to visit, Lucas?"

"Mommy and Daddy. They're taking too long so I left them with Thomas."

Moments later the door opens and in walks, Thomas, Melinda, and Daniel.

Melinda comes over and kisses us both on the cheek. "Congratulations." She turns to Daniel. "I think I've gone a bit overboard with presents, so we'll bring everything up to you in Cape Elizabeth once you are home."

"Thanks, sis."

"That is so cute," Melinda whispers, looking at Lucas being so gentle with his cousin. She retrieves her phone and snaps some photographs of her son and Rose.

"You did good Mack. At least she wasn't as big as Lucas was when he was born. I couldn't sit down properly for weeks."

"I'm not sure I can go through that again," Dean comments, causing me to chuckle as I feel him shudder behind me.

"At least you weren't the one pushing the baby out," Melinda adds as she leans over the new arrival.

I witness Lucas frown before he looks at me and then his mother before his gaze is back on me and Dean. "Auntie Mack, did you really push my cousin out of your—"

"Lucas," Melinda snaps, covering his mouth. "Please behave today, okay?"

He rolls his eyes and tugs his mother's hand away. "What's wrong asking?"

Melinda is quick and seals his lips closed. "Not one more word or we're leaving."

Lucas nods his head. "You're boring." Having the last word, Lucas ignores his mother and concentrates on his cousin.

Dean shakes behind me, so I glance at him and watch as he laughs at our nephew.

Jacob was tired as he climbed into bed beside his wife of nearly seventy years. They'd gotten up that morning looking forward to spending time with Thomas, Mack, and Dean, only to become great grandparents. It had been an emotional day all around, and he wouldn't have changed it for anything.

He considered himself lucky to still be around after ninety plus years, the majority of those spent with the woman who slept silently beside him. She'd been his life from the day that he'd met her, looking windswept out on the cliffs at Two Lights so many years before. When he closed his eyes, he could still see her, and he still felt the jolt of disappointment lace his heart when he heard her brother say she was to be married.

Of course, that hadn't happened, and she'd married him, and their life together had started. They'd had a lot of good years together, each extra day that he got to spend with her was nothing short of a blessing. He was so thankful for the hand that they'd both been dealt, and he had not one regret. How could he? He still had the love of his life beside him...Rose Elizabeth 'Eliza' Evans, his *Rose*.

The End

Character Information

Eleanor ~ although only briefly mentioned in the book, I based her on my great aunt, whose fiancé was killed during the first world war, something that she never recovered from. She spent her remaining years alone, and later in life lived with her brother and sister. She died in 1981.

Lucas ~ at the time of writing this book, my son was six years old, and I knew that I had to base Lucas on him.

Thomas ~ this book is dedicated to my father-in-law who was an avid fisherman, and loved teaching his grandchildren how to bait a hook. He'd travel up to Scotland with his fishing buddies where they'd go out to sea for days on end.

Collier Ship ~ On 3rd March 1947 the Oakey L. Alexander went aground near Cape Elizabeth. This information was researched through the website, www.mainmemory.net

Dear Reader

Thank you for reading *Whispers of Yesterday,* and thank you for your reviews! It's really appreciated.

Subscribe with your email to be alerted about new releases, sales, and events.

lexibuchanan.net

Other books by Author

Hawke's Ridge

Maddox (2025)

Den Hollows

One of Six · Two of Six (2025)

Den of Filth (New MC Series 2025)

Reckless Wilder (2026)

Fifth Realm Series (Romantasy)

Quiver of Chaos · Wings & Arrows (2026)

Standalone Romantasy

Persephone Unchained

Tallulah James Mystery

*Dead and a Murder or Two · Dead and the Wedding Crashers ·
Dead and a Deadly Deed · Dead and a Best Friend*

Boston Bay Vikings

*Camden · Bennett · Ethan · Sutton · Carter · Bryson · Ivan · Theo
· Noah · Knox · Jericho · Roman*

Boston Bay Vikings Minor League

Lake · Rhodes · Nikoli · Dario · Madden · Bradford

Single Titles

Butterflies and Darkness · Come Back to Me · Indecent Villain · Lawful · Love Stryker · Tears in the Rain · Whispers of Yesterday

Holiday Season

Holiday Kisses in the Snow · Jingle Bells

Romantic Suspense Series

Twenty Eight Days · The Next Victim (2025)

Blossom Creek

Christmas at Emelia's · A Rake in Blossom Creek · Heatwave in Blossom Creek · Secret Love in Blossom Creek · Mischief in Blossom Creek · Runaway Bride in Blossom Creek · Naughty & Nice in Blossom Creek

Bad Boy Rockers

My Brother's Girl · Past Sins · My Best Friend's Sister · Never Let Go · Saving Jace · Silent Night (Novella)

Kincaid Sisters

Meant to be Mine · You Were Always Mine · Will You be Mine

McKenzie Brothers

Playing with the Boss · A McKenzie Wedding (Novella) · Playing with Fire · Playing with Desire · Playing with Trouble · Playing with their Hearts · A McKenzie Christmas (Novella)

De La Fuente Family (McKenzie Spinoff)

Love in Montana · Love in Purgatory · Love in Bloom · Love in Country · Love in Flame · Love in Game · Love in Education

McKenzie Cousins

About the Author

While Lexi is the author of the chick lit series, Tallulah James Mystery, and the sexy wild Alaska series, Hawke's Ridge, she also writes romantasy. This author has over seventy published novels. Based in Ireland, this British author has been writing since 2013.

Follow on social media:

Website: https://www.lexibuchanan.com/
Email: authorlexibuchanan@gmail.com

- facebook.com/lexibuchananauthor
- x.com/AuthorLexi
- instagram.com/authorlexib
- bookbub.com/author/lexi-buchanan
- amazon.com/Lexi-Buchanan/e/B009SPA94U